Sweet Memories of Pain & the Future of Pleasure

First Edition

Published by The Nazca Plains Corporation
Las Vegas, Nevada
2007

Dedication

To my fans, friends, and family for their support
these past dozen years.

ISBN: 978-1-934625-22-4

Published by

The Nazca Plains Corporation ®
4640 Paradise Rd, Suite 141
Las Vegas NV 89109-8000

PUBLISHER'S NOTE
Sweet Memories of Pain & the Future of Pleasure is a work of fiction
created wholly by *TammyJo Eckhart's* imagination. All characters are
fictional and any resemblance to any persons living or deceased is purely
by accident. No portion of this book reflects any real person or events.

Cover, Achim Prill
Art Director, Blake Stephens

Sweet Memories of Pain & the Future of Pleasure

TammyJo Eckhart

Contents

A Note from the Author

Has it been so long since I saw my first piece of erotica published? Indeed, that was 1995,[1] and now it's 2007. My first three collections are out of print, and I've regained the rights to some stories from magazines or other anthologies. People have asked me for years where they can get those Amazon stories or that story with the sexy psychopath, and the answer was always: you can't.

Until now.

Four of the five stories in this book were previously published elsewhere but are unavailable to most readers today. Those few copies that go on sale at used bookstores, online or offline, are priced for insane amounts, if you ask me, so now you can just pick up this book and see where my erotica writing began and how it developed between 1995 and 2003.

I've revised each story. Sometimes these changes are minor, but sometimes I've added a new scene or more development of plot and characters. I hope Douglas Adams isn't offended, but he is part of my inspiration for doing this, since he also revised his fiction as the years went along. Perfectionist that I am, I had to do a little bit of something to each tale.

Included in this collection is the two part story about the competing sisters Yvonne and Angelique, whose motivations couldn't be more different.[2] Yvonne was my first "evil" character, and in 1996 she was a way for me to work out some anger that I was dealing with

---

1 "A Day in the Life of the Landfords." *S/M Futures*. Ed. Cecilia Tan. Boston: Circlet Press, Inc., 1995, pp 1-24.

2 "Punishment for the Crime" originally published in *Punishment for the Crime*. New York: Masquerade Books, Inc., June 1996, pp. 41-98 and "Justice" originally published in *Justice and other short erotic tales*. San Francisco: Greenery Press, 1999, pp. 39-77.

from my past. While I considered Yvonne to be pure evil, emails I received from readers and conversations I had in person taught me a valuable lesson: readers will interpret things their own way, and Yvonne was turning on a fair number of people.

Even when using my writing to work out my own thoughts and past, which I think many writers do, I always need something more to drive my creativity. In this case I had just finished reading the Constitution of the United States of America. Since I study slavery throughout human history, I was particularly intrigued by the 13th Amendment and how as a nation we basically ignore one part of it. What if we didn't ignore it? What if slavery was used as a punishment for criminals; how would or could that play out? If I had an evil interpretation of this amendment, could I have a good interpretation of it as well? I think that Angelique in 1999 shows that the law can indeed be used by people of all moral and ethical motivations. Motivation is really what separates those of us doing BDSM from rapists, abusers, and users, after all, right?

In 1997, between the two parts of the sister tale, I published a collection which re-imagined the tragic legends about Amazons written by the ancient Greeks and Romans. While I am very proud of what that collection did — it represented stories from the classical world in appropriate yet modern ways — they were all tragic and thus difficult to choose from. I want to thank Janine, Bridget, and the men in my life for their feedback on these stories. All of them thought that "Journey Unto Warrior"[3] was the best from that seven story anthology. I think the story is multifaceted, using comedy, torture, social rules, and individual choices to create something my readers at the time called simply "hot." I did make an attempt to use Greek names and terms for some things, but it is not an attempt to be historically accurate; take one of my college classes if you want that.

Ever wonder what might happen if a voyeur had the tables turned? I wondered about that myself when I was asked to contribute a story to Greenery Press's charity anthology back in 2003. I decided to play out this question aboard a spaceship in "Captain's Gaze"[4] as Jay uses his

---

3 Originally published in *Amazons: Erotic Explorations of the Ancient Myths*. New York: Masquerade Books, Inc., July 1997, pp. 239-266.

4 Originally published in *Dreaming in Color: a special edition anthology of erotic writing by Greenery Press authors*. Oakland: Greenery Press, 2003, pp.39-51.

conservative mistress's own reluctance for their mutual enjoyment. As many of my stories do, this one examines how unrealistic it is to think that power lies only with the owner or that it is unsubmissive to desire and act upon one's desires. Power flows between both people; it is authority that determines the nature of the dynamic.

I love vampires. I give every new television show and movie a chance if it has a vampire, and I'm a huge fan of the RPG *Vampire: the Masquerade,* which I have run during several summers and at some conventions. I particularly love the idea of the vampires' slaves or retainers, though I also have tales devoted to showing a vampire in the submissive position. I can't say that I've been inspired by any one legend or work of fiction about vampires, since they all have wonderful potential, because they cross that final boundary between life and death. For the first time I want to present my vampire piece called *Doll*, which explores the competition and the limits of sexuality in the world of the living undead. I know my audiences adore *Circle of Blood* from *Eroscapes* when I read it to them, so I hope this twist on the vampire pleases them all as much.

The title of this collection was difficult for me. Entirely new work seems easy to title: find a theme, or choose one of the stories from the anthology. My mind drew a blank on this project, so I turned to my Yahoo! group fan site and several online BDSM groups of which I am an active member, as well as my friends and family. Lauri suggested the winning title which I used with minor modifications to make it flow a bit better.

A special thanks to my friend Emilie for her reading of the entire book. Her careful thoughts on each story helped me revise them in a few places. Her enjoyment of them confirmed what I had hoped: This is not just a collection for the kinky but for anyone who enjoys fiction with strong women and intense situations.

If you like what you read, please consider writing a review on Amazon.com or other bookstores, and please tell your friends about my work. If you are ever at a convention I'm attending, do seek me out, because I love signing books and talking to people. If you are a member of a BDSM club or science fiction/fantasy/horror organization, send me a line; I might be able to attend your events, and I love reading to audiences.

    Now turn the page, and start visiting my erotic worlds.

Punishment for the Crime

"Are you sure you want to see him? He hasn't been tamed yet." General Corriger pointed out to her liege lady as they walked through the slave barracks.

"I feel like a challenge, Valerie." Yvonne, heir to the remains of what had been New England in the reconstituted United Eastern States, stopped at one of the cells and snapped her fingers in front of the bars. The man inside hurried to her, kneeling and licking her fingers. "I believe you have broken all of these slaves. I think I deserve a little fun too."

"I agree, though I thought the raid we're planning would provide that."

"It's fun, but it's almost too easy."

The two continued through the barracks to the palace in silence. When they reached the princess' second suite, her "guest" quarters as she called them, the general opened the door, saying, "He's a drug dealer, Yvonne."

"I know." She crossed to her desk, where she removed her helmet.

"He's gone through three owners since the sentencing five years ago."

"I know," Yvonne ran her fingers through her shoulder length bright red hair.

"He has a record that's pages long."

"I know." She sat down in the plain oak chair in the center of the room. "He is the best challenge since the system was put into effect fifty years ago. I read the reports claiming he can't be broken. I don't believe it. The right methods haven't been used."

"And you know the right methods?"

"I think I do." She raised her hand as footsteps and curses approached. "I think that's him now."

The general nodded and stood slightly behind the chair.

"Enter!" Yvonne yelled before the knock came.

Two guards entered with a struggling man. His clothes, which had been new for the auction, were torn and bloody from his resistance. He blinked and cursed when the blindfold was removed. "Fuck! Turn down the Goddamn lights!"

Yvonne sat silently as the guards forced him to his knees. Each guard placed her foot on his calves. "He's been like this the entire transport, your highness," one of the guards explained.

General Corriger stepped up to him, grabbing his long black hair to force him to face the princess. "This is your new mistress. You will obey her every command."

He looked the young, beautiful woman sitting in front of him slowly over. "I know what you need, your highness," he said with a sneer.

"You son of a bitch!" The general raised her fist to strike him but was stopped by a shake of her liege lady's head.

Yvonne waved her hand.

"Are you sure?" the general asked. After another wave of the princess' hand, the general turned to the guards. "We're dismissed."

The guard released the man, who jumped to his feet and watched them leave. He turned to the woman seated on the chair. "They didn't lock the door. What's to stop me from leaving?"

When the woman didn't answer, he reached for the door. Immediately his body was struck with electricity that made him scream. He released the doorknob and staggered away. The woman was now reading from a folder and didn't even glance at him. He hurried to the windows only to find them barred and a guard smiling back at him from a balcony.

"We are five stories up," the woman replied calmly.

After examining the entire room he started to approach her from behind. Suddenly, his shirt was pinned to the wall by a dagger.

"Such a pity to have to ruin that lovely shirt," the woman replied as she came and pulled it out. She returned to the chair. "Do you know who I am?"

"You mean besides a bitch?" he replied, walking to where he could see her face clearly. "No, I don't, and I don't really care."

"Look at this;" she threw him her helmet with the royal crest. "My parents named me Yvonne."

He caught the helmet and recognized the crest and the name. "You're the Butcher?" He shook his head to clear his mind of the images of slaughter he had seen on the streets for years, the prostitutes, druggies and dealers dead in the street every night in the big cities. "You can't be; that was years ago."

"Call them my reckless teenage years." She picked up the folder and opened it. "You are called Jake."

"That's my name; don't wear it out."

"Convicted on several accounts of petty crime since the age of ten until your sentencing for drug dealing five years ago. That would make you twenty-five now. Do you enjoy being a slave, Jake?"

"Oh, sure. It's a blast. What the fuck kind of question is that?"

"You desire to be a slave, Jake. The laws have been quite clear since before you were born."

He remained silent for a moment as his mind worked through the churning her words caused in his stomach. Then he tried to reclaim some control, "Hey, the collar and tattoos removed. I'm not marked a slave anymore, you can't keep me here."

"You have to earn those symbols of slavery."

"Oh, and I suppose I'm gonna beg you for them, right?"

"Yes. Right now, in fact." She sat up straight in the chair. "On your knees."

He approached slowly and bent down so they were face to face. "Fuck you!"

She stood up and he backed up a few steps. She picked up her helmet. "I will be on campaign a few days. This is your room. Do what you want. You will be taken care of as you deserve." Without further words she opened the door and left.

Jake hurried after her, but the door closed in his face. Electricity shot through him as he grabbed the doorknob again. He backed off and nodded his head. "It's no big deal, lady! You can torture me all you want, but it won't work!"

Yvonne entered her second suite after four days on campaign. She had showered and changed into her dress uniform for the supper she would be attending shortly. The convicted drug dealer walked up to her angrily as she closed the door.

"What the fuck is going on here?"

"Is sometime wrong? You look clean, new clothes, haircut, face smooth. What's the problem?"

"They haven't brought me any food since you left!"

"Oh, I'm so sorry."

He glanced at her shiny uniform and her calm, even somewhat concerned face. "So, you'll tell them to feed me?"

"I don't have any control over who gets fed here."

"What you fucking mean you don't have control? You're heir to the throne, aren't you?"

"Only four types of people are fed around here. The family, the guests, the staff, and the slaves," she stated flatly.

Jake ran his hand through his spiky hair. "I see what you're trying to do. But it's not going to work."

Yvonne nodded. "I'm off to a dinner now. Good evening," she added, closing the door behind her.

Jake threw himself against the door and was shocked once more. He sat where the electricity had thrown him and stared at the door in anger.

Jake stood looking out the bars of the double doors to the balcony. The guard there didn't interfere with his looking out over the main entrance and road. He had gotten up early every day since he'd last seen her to shave and try to look his best. Since anger didn't work, maybe a little charm would.

"It's been a hell of a week, otherwise I would have been here sooner."

He turned at the sound of her voice. She was dressed in a black negligée and robe, black slippers on her feet. He checked his voice and manner before approaching her. "I was hoping you would come."

"Really?" she folded her arms.

"Yes, of course." He stopped at a few feet from her. "Has anyone ever told you how beautiful you are?"

"Many people."

Jake paused to reconsider this approach. He started to unbutton his shirt. "You've had a busy week. I bet I can help you relax, your highness."

She laughed out loud at him for a moment before shaking her head. "I'm leaving tomorrow morning to tour some prison camps. I may be gone several weeks." She glanced at the ground directly in front of her feet then into his eyes. "Is there anything you need before I go?"

His eyes darkened in hate. "No."

Yvonne left without a word.

"It isn't working, is it?" the general asked after her liege lady had closed the door behind her.

Yvonne put her arm around the other woman. "It's working quite well. Just as I planned, in fact." She unclasped one of the buckles on the general's breastplate. "We don't need to sleep for a few hours. Come with me."

The general took the hand that had moved to her neck. She passionately kissed it. "It would be my pleasure."

Jake dragged himself from the bed. He looked in the bathroom mirror at his cheekbones, clearly visible now. He took off the shirt he had fallen asleep in and counted his ribs. He drank a glass of water and brushed his teeth. He sank to the floor, unable once again to step into the shower. He crawled from habit and turned the water on cold. This woke him up enough to shave. He crawled to the double doors and opened them slightly. "Please. How long?"

The guard shook her head. "You should be branded and collared."

"Please?" For the first time his voice really sounded pitiful.

"Twenty-one days since she was last here."

Jake crawled from the balcony and managed to lift his head up to the bed to rest there. *Thirty-two days without food. Oh, God. Why didn't she just stab me that first day?* He heard the door opening and waited for the guards to come in. For the past week they had come, and the last six days he hadn't been strong enough to fight them off. "Please?" he whispered as they picked him up and threw him on the bed on his stomach.

They laughed as they pulled his pants from him and forced his legs apart. "You're nothing. Only family, guest, staff and slaves don't get raped around here. You're nothing."

After the guards had finished, he managed to pull up his pants. *No blood again.* He was trying to turn himself over when the door opened again.

Yvonne walked in and over to the bed. She had come straight from reporting to her father, so she was still dusty from the ride. "You look like shit."

Jake reached for her hand. "Please?" His eyes begged.

Yvonne cocked one eye and stepped back a little. She waited for a full minute. "I've just come to tell you I've been called away on political business up north so I'll not see you for a week or more..."

"Please..." he hurled himself from the bed to her feet. He groveled at her feet. "Mistress, please," he whispered.

She stepped back a few paces. "What did you say?"

He crawled until his head rested in front of her boots, his body flat against the floor. "Mistress, please."

"Only my slaves are allowed to use that title for me."

Jake swallowed his last shreds of pride. "Please allow me to wear your collar and your mark."

"I thought you were dead set against being a slave." She walked to the chair and sat down.

Jake crawled to her feet and prostrated himself there. "Please. You were right..."

"Right about what?" she said, leaning closer to him.

"You said I must want to be a slave, otherwise I wouldn't have dealt drugs. You're right, Mistress. Please allow me the honor to be your slave. I'll do anything, no matter the job," he added.

"You're not worth the honor of shoveling shit in the barn around here."

He started to weep softly. "Please, please then just kill me."

Yvonne bent and ran her fingers through his hair, then gripped it tightly in her fist and yanked his head up. He didn't struggle at all as she placed the dagger to his throat. "Being my slave means complete obedience to me and me alone. Obedience without question or hesitation. Obedience to any and everything that I command. Obedience to my unspoken commands and desires. Nothing will exist for you but me."

"I don't exist except for you, Mistress," he managed to yell in his terror.

"Who doesn't exist?"

He swallowed and ventured again. "Jake doesn't exist except for you, Mistress. Please."

She removed her knife and released his hair. "Lick the dust off my boots, and make them shine."

Jake slowly started to lick the right boot. The dust almost made him cough and gag, but he continued. By the time the first boot was shining, he moved with eagerness to the next boot. He recalled her words and burned them into his mind, 'Being my slave means complete obedience to me and me alone.' *To you alone, to you alone.*

When the other boot was finished, Yvonne pushed him aside and went to the door. He scramble to his knees in fear, but dared not speak. "Guards!" The guards entered and stood at attention. "Take him and follow me!"

Jake tried to walk between the guards so their grip on his arms wasn't so painful. He was taken to a dank dark room several stories down. He was thrust into a chair while the guards held him.

Yvonne disappeared while a man in a dirty apron approached him. He measured his neck. "He's emaciated. I'll add a little for him to grow." The man looked at the metal strips hanging along the wall. "Type?"

"Gold plated," Yvonne's voice called from the other room.

The smith placed a two-inch strip around his neck. "Don't move, or you could die." He fired his blowtorch on low and soldered the two ends of the metal together. Jake would have flinched when the flame grazed him, but he didn't have the energy. He suspected the smith had done it on purpose.

The guards then lifted him from the chair and carried him to the other room. One held his arms as the other loosened his pants and stripped him to the waist. They bent him over a table and strapped his arms and legs to it before leaving the room.

Yvonne stepped into his sight. She held a smoking branding iron in her hand. "We don't tattoo. We brand our property. This is your last chance."

He felt the sweat drip down his forehead into one of his eyes. He lowered his head to the table. "Jake doesn't exist except for you, Mistress," he stated again. He couldn't hold back his scream as the iron burned into his buttocks.

"Guards!" Yvonne replaced the iron down and gripped her slave by the hair. He was barely conscious from the pain. "Take him to the steward. I want him fed, cleaned, clothed, and shown the palace and grounds. After a night of sleep, I want him brought to my office by nine sharp."

The guards nodded, unstrapped the slave and carried him away.

Jake followed the steward through the palace. He had to keep reminding himself that there was no way out now so he would stop looking for one. "Let's rest a minute. OK?"

The steward paused with distaste. "You have no stamina."

"You try not eating for a month and see how much stamina you have." The cockiness was returning to Jake's voice.

"You brought that upon yourself. Perhaps you need to be reminded of that," the steward threatened as he stepped closer to the drug dealer.

Jake stood up slowly, wincing at the pain in his buttocks. "I'm not going to punch you out, because my mistress ordered me to follow you. So lead the way."

Jake was escorted to her office, which he remembered from his tour was near the throne room. "Hey," he started before they reached the door, "any advice for me?"

The guards' laughter sent chills through him as he recognized them as his rapists. They opened the door and pushed him in.

He stood there in front of her desk, unsure what to do. She didn't glance at him, but only at the computer screen. He looked at the clock on the wall. *One minute to nine. Nine o'clock. Why isn't she noticing me?* He knelt on one knee, then the other. After another minute he prostrated himself flat on the floor in front of her desk. He held his breath as her boots moved from under her desk and reappeared in front of his face.

She didn't speak but simply tapped one toe once. He swallowed quickly and moved to that boot. He licked it slowly until it shone, then moved to the other boot. "Stand up."

He rose to his feet and looked her straight in the eyes. He was knocked to the floor by her blow.

"Stand up."

He rose to his feet but focused his eyes on the second button of her shirt. He was knocked to the floor by her blow. He touched his lips and tasted blood.

"Stand up."

He rose again to his feet. He stood straight and focused his eyes over her shoulder. He felt her walk slowly around him. He didn't fight as she moved his hands, arms, and legs. When she squeezed his raw butt cheek, he sucked his breath in through his teeth.

Yvonne sat on the edge of her desk and admired him for a moment. "You lost some weight, but you'll get it back. I see he burned your neck. Do you think he meant to?"

"Perhaps." He saw her start to stand up. "Perhaps, Mistress," he added quickly. He saw her smile and nod.

"You will follow me today and every day until I tire of your presence. We don't sell our property. When that time comes you will be given away as a gift or killed." Her words made Jake swallow but he was smart enough to not reply as she stood up.

He followed her out of the office and into the throne room. *She is very straight with me, at least.* He stayed about three paces behind her. She stood, glancing at her watch until an older gentleman and lady entered. On their heads were the crowns of the realm. He recognized them from the all the money he had handled from his years on the streets.

"Father, Mother." Yvonne embraced them both. She turned to the slave behind her. "I told you I could tame him."

Their majesties glanced at each other and their daughter. The queen approached the slave, who stood his ground but did not look her in the eye. "He seems a lovely lad. A little thin."

"That was necessary, Mother."

"If you say so, my dear." The queen held out her hand.

"Kiss her ring," Yvonne whispered.

He bowed low and barely touched the queen's ring with his lips. He remained bowed until told to rise by the queen. "Jake, your majesty," he replied softly to her inquiry.

"He seems quite well mannered to me," the queen stated as she moved aside for her husband.

"Looks can be deceiving. But you know that." His speech was obviously directed toward his daughter.

"I don't trust him at all, Father. He hasn't earned that yet," Yvonne walked up behind her father and glared at the slave. "Tell my Father who you are."

Jake avoided both their eyes as he repeated the words. "Jake doesn't exist except for you, Mistress."

The king held out his ring hand and nodded as the slave bowed and kissed it. "Watch him, my dear. Now," the king turned to his daughter with a smile, "it's about time for petitions. Shall we go, my girls?"

Yvonne followed their majesties to the three thrones and sat at her father's right hand. Jake stationed himself behind and to the right of the throne.

Jake tried to listen with interest to the cases brought before the royal court. He hadn't been fed that morning; the steward's excuse had been that she hadn't specifically ordered him to. His stomach growled softly. He saw her fist clench and feared she had heard. His interest was piqued when a man was dragged into court by some cops. *Eddy? Oh, shit, dude.*

The man was defending himself against his drug use and dealing conviction. The punishment for this was death, because the theory went that enslaving someone who was already a slave to drugs wasn't a deterrent. Yvonne motioned to Jake, who knelt by her side, and moved his head close to hers. "Know him?"

"Unfortunately." After a second she had her hand around his throat. "Yes, Mistress," he croaked. His throat was released. He remained by her side.

"I have a question." Yvonne stood to speak. She walked toward the defendant. "Mr. Nole, do you recognize that man," she said, pointing to her slave.

The druggy shook his head quickly.

"Jake, come stand before the defendant so he can get a closer look at you." She waited until the slave stood directly before the other man. "Look at him closely, Mr. Nole."

The man glared at the slave and mouthed something to him.

"What did that man say to you?" Yvonne asked.

"He said 'traitor,' Mistress."

"You fucking bastard!" The defendant tried to beat the slave, but was pulled off him by the cops.

Jake took a deep breath and glanced at his mistress. She returned to her throne saying, "Feel free to ask him any questions, counselors."

"Yes." The prosecution stepped forward. "May he stay on the floor for the questioning, Your Highness?"

"As long as you need him," she replied as she seated herself.

"What is your name?"

"Jake Monroe."

"Social security number?"

Jake paused to think, then rattled off the nine numbers.

After a moment both attorneys had copies of his record. "You were sentenced to open market slavery five years ago for drug dealing. Is that correct?"

"Yes," Jake folded his arms angrily, remembering his own trial.

"Do you know the defendant?"

"Yes, unfortunately."

"Why unfortunately?"

"We had the same supplier, but he used to do more dope than

he sold, so they cut him off. He started coming around begging me for some. He even stole a kilo from me once."

"Would you consider Mr. Nole to be an honest person just needing medical attention?"

"No," Jake snorted. "He's the type of guy that would sell his birth mother for a capsule of speed."

The prosecution turned to the defense lawyer. "Your witness."

"You were sent to reform school several times, weren't you?"

"Yes."

The lawyer smiled icily. "You've been sold four times since your conviction for drug dealing, haven't you?"

"Yes."

"You are a liar, a thief, and a scam artist, aren't you?"

Jake brought his hands down to his sides in fists. Out of the corner of his eye he saw his mistress lean forward in her seat. "Yes," he whispered angrily.

The lawyer smiled and nodded. "No further questions."

The prosecution lawyer nodded and dismissed the slave. Jake returned to his place behind his mistress' throne.

"Hey, yo! What's to eat around here?" Jake walked into the main kitchen through the slaves' entrance.

A young woman approached him. Her slave collar was thin and made of iron. "Why didn't you report at feeding time?"

"I get time to eat when the princess tells me it's time to eat. I have thirty minutes tops."

"I'll make you a sandwich then. The milk is in the fridge over there, and the glasses are in the cupboard next to it." The girl opened another refrigerator and got out bread, meat, cheese and butter.

"Aren't you a little young to be sentenced to slavery?" he asked, sitting down at the table to watch her make the sandwich.

"My mother was convicted of giving AIDS to three of her johns. She was in the hospital at the time of the sentence, so I took her place so she could get health care."

"Your mother gave AIDS to royalty?"

The girl handed him the sandwich. "No, the royal family heard about our case and interceded on my behalf. I would probably be dead by now if they hadn't."

Jake nodded as he chewed. *Victims' families can be bitches.* "How long you been here?"

"Four years."

"How old are you?"

"Sixteen. How old are you?"

"Twenty-five."

"Why are you a slave?"

Jake paused to finish his sandwich before replying. "Drug dealing." He expected the girl to yell at him or even physically attack him. Most slaves did when they found out what he had done, the exception being other drug dealers. Dealers were constantly blamed for all the problems of the world not those who sought them out for a fix; it was all unfair as far as Jake was concerned but his thoughts didn't change reality. Instead the young slave just walked quietly away from him. Jake finished his milk, rinsed it out over the sink and drank a glass of water to clear his throat. "Where's the toilet?"

The girl pointed to a small door, then ran from the room in tears.

Jake hurried from the kitchen through the corridors. He slowed down when he spotted a clock. *Ten minutes. I can stroll back.* He stopped by one of the windows to get an unobstructed view of the main entrance. *This place is fucking huge.* He slowly continued through the corridors until he reached the main dinning room. He slid in through the slaves' entrance and took his position three paces behind his mistress' chair. *Two minutes early.*

He stood there listening to the dull conversation until she set her napkin aside. He moved to her chair and pulled it back as she stood.

"I think I'll be dining alone tonight, if you don't mind?" Yvonne asked her parents.

"Of course, darling," the queen said as the king merely nodded. "You need some vacation time."

"Thank you both." Yvonne turned on her heel and left the room. She walked quickly down the hall and to the elevator that took them to the ground floor.

She entered a different room from any he had seen yesterday. He followed her to a bench and recognized the gear stored there as riding gear. When she sat down he knelt before her.

"Boots," stated simply.

He got the boots by the bench. After removing the others she wore, he placed these on her feet. Next he helped her into her jacket and handed her the riding crop that she promptly struck his cheek with. He stood there a moment, then fell to his knees at her feet. "Mistress?..." he stopped before saying anything further.

"The horses need exercise, and so do you. While I am riding you will run along the racetrack four times. That's two miles."

Jake looked up at her in shock and received another lash from the riding crop. "Yes, Mistress." He followed her out of the building to the early spring air. He shivered in his simple shirt, pants and shoes.

"You'll warm up." She left him at the track and took her horse from the groom who came out.

After she was out of earshot, he spoke to the groom. "Can you believe that she wants me to run two miles on that track?"

"That's four laps," the groom replied. "You don't look like you're in very good shape. You better get started. She only rides for half an hour."

"Thanks for the sympathy," Jake replied as the groom returned to the stables. He headed to the track.

He saw her returning as he finishing vomiting from the four laps. He wiped his mouth on his hand, which he then wiped on the grass. He walked as quickly as he could back to her.

Yvonne glanced at him. "That's what you get for not eating for a month," she told him bluntly. "Show him the bathroom, Mike," she ordered the groom.

Jake followed the man to a small bathroom where he was able to vomit again. Afterwards he rinsed out his mouth, drank a little water and used the toilet. The groom showed him where his mistress' ready room was. She was standing there in her riding gear waiting for him. He removed her jacket when she turned her back to him and changed her boots when she sat.

"Time for a snack," she announced.

They went back through the corridors of the palace to the main kitchen. The girl he'd met before was there and bowed low when they entered. "What do you have that's good for a snack, Betty?"

"My Lady, baking was done yesterday so there are many types of breads, cookies and pies." The girl wiped off the table and pulled out a chair for the princess.

"Bring an assortment of cookies and two glasses of milk." After the girl had bowed and left, Yvonne kicked a chair out from the table. "Use that as your table, Jake. You look like you need some food too."

"Thank you, Mistress," he said kneeling by it.

"Sit down and join me, Betty," Yvonne said when the girl returned with a platter of cookies and two mugs of milk. "Let's talk."

The girl giggled and sat down opposite the princess. She waited until Yvonne had handed her slave several cookies and bitten into one herself before taking one. "I made the sugar cookies and the peanut butter ones," Betty whispered.

"You are a great cook," Yvonne said with a smile. "You're going to make someone a good spouse someday."

The girl set the cookie down and sadly looked at the table.

"You'll be eighteen in least than two years. I'll convince my father to let you marry and live out on the land. Don't you believe me?"

The girl looked up with tears in her eyes. "Oh, yes, My Lady. It just seems so far away at times."

Yvonne nodded slowly. "You should start looking around for a mate. Let me know if you're interested in anyone and I'll arrange some meetings." She leaned across the table. "Anyone caught your eye yet?"

Betty blushed. "Well, there's the groom, the younger one. Sometimes when he comes to get their meals I see him smiling at me," she whispered.

"Mike?" Yvonne nodded and finished her milk. "I'll arrange for you to take a few evening meals out at the stables so you can visit with each other."

Jake stood quickly and pulled her chair back so she could stand.

What the fuck? One minute yelling and hitting and the next arranging nice things. Maybe I should have just starved to death. He shook his head slightly to clear his mind.

"You met this character?" Yvonne asked the girl with a nod at her slave.

The girl frowned. "Yes. He ate lunch in here."

"You don't like him." Yvonne suddenly turned to him and grabbed him by the hair, forcing his head on the table. "Drug dealers are the scum of world. Tell him why your mother was a hooker."

"This bastard laced her drink at a restaurant. He got her hooked on it and made her turn tricks to get the stuff. " The girl's voice dripped venom with each word.

Jake stood up when his hair was released. "I'm sorry, but I didn't force my product on anyone." He waited in silence as the girl gathered the platter and mugs and walked away. When he felt his mistress turn to go he followed three paces behind her.

They went to the fourth floor and stopped in front of elaborate double doors. "This is my suite. You know the way through the slaves' entrance but just in case you have to escort a guest to me you should know what it looks like from out here." She opened the door and entered.

Jake followed. He looked around the room, then stopped himself and just stood at attention after she shut the door.

"Go ahead. Look around," she said, then disappeared down a small hallway.

The suite looked as if it rose two stories. There was a spiral staircase in one corner. An embroidered divan and chairs sat before a low table. Full bookcases lined the walls. He walked down the hallway after her. She stepped aside to let him look in the restroom. He followed her back out to the main room.

"This is where I receive guests. If you have to bring someone to see me, you bring them here." She climbed the stairs. "This is where I live when I'm home."

Jake looked at the much darker room decorated in blacks and reds. He was at first startled by the weapons that lined the walls. *This is more like what the Butcher should have.* He waited at the foot of the stairs for her to wave her hand for him to look around. He found a full bathroom, also dark and foreboding. Three huge sliding doors displayed her clothes. Another smaller unit held clothing she said would be his. He closed the door and returned to the main room to find her sitting on the four-poster bed. It was enormous and covered with a blood red quilt. He knelt at her feet and removed her boots, which he carried back to her closet where all the shoes had been.

Yvonne reclined on the bed staring at him as he stood silently at attention. She sat up at the sound of a bell. "You will exit through the slave corridors, get our dinner and return with it the same way. When I am not eating with my family or guests, you will get every meal. Unless you are otherwise occupied," she added with a half smile.

"Yes, Mistress," Jake bowed and hurried through the slaves' entrance. He paused after the door closed behind him to stare at it. *Handcuffs?* He hurried through the narrow corridors to the kitchen. *Thank god for the signs.* He hurried into the hall and first met the girl Betty. "I'm here to get the princess' dinner."

"It's over there on the table."

"Thank you," Jake took the large gold tray that held three covered plates, two goblets and a bottle of wine. "I'll bring it back when she's finished."

One of the cooks shook his head. "No, no. You just leave it outside the slaves' entrance and I'll send someone to pick it up."

Jake nodded. "Sure." He hurried as quickly as he could through the corridors. *Wonder if I'll get to eat.* His stomach growled as the tasty fumes rose from the platter. He realized gratefully that the door to her suite swung inwards, so he backed his way in.

"Set it on that small table then bring the table here," her voice ordered him.

The room was darker now because the sun was setting. He brought the table to her. He stepped back when he saw she was dressed in the same negligée she had worn weeks earlier when he had attempted to seduce her.

"Pour two glasses of wine. You'll be eating with me."

He knelt on the floor by the bed and filled both goblets. He handed one to her and sipped his own. As she ate she would hand him various bits of food that he quickly licked from her fingers. He noticed she was careful to only give him the bland foods and not pieces dipped in the rich cream sauce that rested in a bowl next to the meat dish. When she finished the main meal, she uncovered the dessert -- a small chocolate torte covered with chocolate curls.

"Sit up and face me."

He turned and knelt so his face was directly in her view but carefully focused his eyes over her shoulder.

"Close your eyes. Are you afraid of me?"

He paused for a second then whispered, "Yes, Mistress."

"Good. Open your mouth."

He opened it widely and felt something enter it.

"Close your mouth."

He felt metal, then felt it sliding from his mouth. *Chocolate.* He started to bite, but felt a cold metal prick right above his collar. He waited for the word.

"Eat it."

He bit into the torte and chewed it slowly before swallowing.

"Who are you?"

He could felt her breathe on his cheek. "Jake doesn't exist except for you, Mistress." He felt her move away.

After a few moments she spoke. "Take your clothes off, slowly."

He opened his eyes and was thrown to the floor by her fist.

"Take your clothes off slowly," she repeated.

Keeping his eyes closed he stood and slipped out of the shoes. He bent each leg up to remove the socks. He paused between each button on his shirt then slowly let it slide off his shoulders. *I can't look too good now.* He unbuttoned the pants and stepped out of them. The bikini briefs fell to the floor.

"You can ask me one question every night and I'll answer honestly. What's your question for tonight?"

Jake kept his eyes closed and asked, "How did you know that starving me would break me?"

"I read your history in your legal file. All of it. Never doubt that I know how to handle you and what makes you tick," she warned him.

He waited naked in the cold of the room for the entire night.

Jake followed the guards through the slave corridors. They stopped in front of the infirmary. He went in and found a man and woman sitting reading magazines. "Where's the medic?"

"We're them," the woman replied, setting aside the magazine. "How can we help you?"

"I was sent by Princess Yvonne. "I'm Jake Monroe. Princess Yvonne's slave," he added slowly when the woman just stared at him.

"The one she starved, huh?" the man said as he stood. "I'll go get the file."

"Yeah. She wants to see if I'm in good health," Jake threw the words out and sat down on the chair the man had abandoned.

The woman stood up and was about to speak when the man returned. "Let's look and see what she wants done," the woman said, flipping open the folder. "A full exam. Guess he's yours, John."

"OK." The man pointed to a door. "In there, and take all your clothes off."

Jake rose slowly and went through the doors. *Typical exam room.* He took his clothes off and sat on the exam table. "Come in," he said when the knock came on the door.

The male doctor entered with a shy smile. "This is only my second month here. Says on your chart that you're new too." The doctor frowned. "Says you were denied food for thirty-two days. Whatever you did, I'd suggest that you'll not do it again. That's not good for your body. Let's weigh you first."

Jake got on the scale. He looked at himself in the mirror next to the scale. *I look pretty good now.*

"You're regained most of the weight you lost. About three pounds less than your weigh-in. Let's check the body fat."

Jake hurried to Yvonne's office after his exam. He knocked on the door before entering. She was speaking to two gentlemen, who ignored him as he entered, and stood behind her chair three paces. He kept his eyes forward and listened silently. When Yvonne moved her cup toward him, he went and got the tea set. He poured her another cup and silently offered the gentlemen more.

After about an hour, the gentlemen rose and left. Yvonne remained in her seat looking over her fingertips. After a moment she moved to rise. Jake slid her chair back and replaced it when she walked to the window. He waited silently by her desk.

"Give me the doctor's report," she commanded, holding out her hand.

Jake took the envelope from his back pocket and handed it to her. He waited by the window while she read.

"Good," she stated softly. She left through the slaves' entrance.

Jake followed her through the corridors to her main suite's slave entrance.

"Hold out your hands," she ordered turning to face him. She fastened the cuffs over one of his wrists.

Jake followed her into the room and removed his clothes when ordered. She dialed the kitchen on her phone and told them to bring lunch, dinner and breakfast up to her room. He stood silently as she lifted his hands over his head and fastened them over a rod that appeared from the ceiling. She moved his legs two feet apart and strapped them to the floor. Then she disappeared down the hallway to return a few minutes later with a small suitcase.

Yvonne opened the suitcase and laid it on the bed. "Your question gets to come early today. What is it?" She removed her jacket and took off her tie.

Jake looked straight at her; he had learned that this was allowed during his question-time. "Why are you doing this?"

"What do you think I'm going to do to you?" She looked through the suitcase.

"You can do whatever you want to me at any time. But I think you're going to torture me and I want to know why," he asked, then jerked back in anticipation of a slap.

"I am angry about the meeting, about the war. You're going to help me get rid of that anger." She approached and placed a blindfold over his eyes. "Don't fight it and you might enjoy it."

She pressed a few buttons in a hidden panel and raised the rod so he was stretched taunt. First she simply walked around him, touching him with a feather every now and then. The feather's touch became more frequent until he was gasping from laughter and pain.

"Please, Mistress..." he flinched from the touch but couldn't move far. "I can't... breathe."

"Who can't breathe?" she asked, increasing the touches so he couldn't answer for several seconds. "Who can't breathe?" she repeated, slowing her tickling.

"Jake... can't... breathe... Mistress... please." He cursed inwardly at forgetting to only refer to himself in the third person in her presence.

"You have to breathe," she said and stood back.

Jake tried to control his gasps as his body stopped sending double signals to his brain. Just as his breathing returned to normal he jumped from the feather's return to his rib cage. "Oh, please," he gasped. *What's going on? No, it can't be.* He felt his penis start to rise. "Please... no... please."

"I don't think you want me to stop," she whispered. "I can see that you like it," she added, running the feather over his now long shaft.

"Oohhh..." he shook his head, wishing he could thrust. Suddenly she stopped. He listened closely and heard her open the slave door. She set something on the small table.

"Time to eat," she announced.

He felt his arms lowered a bit. Next he felt his ankles unstrapped. His arms were further lowered so he had to kneel in order not to be hit on the head with the rod. He blinked as the blindfold was removed. The light indicated she had opened the curtains; the light breeze indicated open balcony doors.

She unlocked one of the handcuffs, which allowed him to lower his arms. He took the sandwich she handed him and ate it in silence. He ate another sandwich and an apple and washed it down with a mug of spiced wine. He went to the bathroom to empty himself and brush his teeth as commanded. When he returned the food platter was gone, and she waited by the now higher rod.

He raised his hands and felt the other cuff locked around the wrist. Without a word, he spread his legs and felt the strap placed around his ankles. *If it gets her off to tickle me, it's no tough job. Here it comes,* he thought as the blindfold was tied over his eyes. "Aahhh!" he screamed as something cut through the back of his knees. He regained his posture after a few seconds passed and he realized that his knees were still there.

The blow landed on his buttocks. Whack! Whack! Whack! Then a pause. The next blow fell across his shoulders. Whack! *Staff... wooden.* His mind registered what the weapon might be. Five years of fighting his sentence had given him experience with many instruments of torture. He started to count the blows to focus his mind. After he reached ninety-four, the blows stopped. His skin felt hot and he could feel welts rising. Sweat dripped down his face.

"You like this. I knew you would," Yvonne touched his hot cock with one of her fingers and was rewarded by his moan. "I can feel the anger slowly start to leave me."

Swish, crack! He tried to bend over to protect his chest but only found his arms lifted higher by the rod. Swish, crack! *Whip.* Swish, crack! "Yip!" he squealed as the next blow struck his nipple. The blows stopped when he reached twenty-seven, all on his front.

"Please," he gasped. A moment later his mouth and throat were filled with something hard. *Leather; must be a gag of some type.* He braced himself for the next blows. These came on his back. SWISH, CRACK! He tried to scream and almost gagged on the object in his throat. SWISH, CRACK! He counted forty-eight more before they stopped. His sweat flowed freely now, and he felt the unmistakable trickle of blood on his back.

His ankles were freed as his arms were raised so he hung limp above the floor. He felt himself swinging backwards for a few feet. He thrashed in the handcuffs as the icy water hit him. Twice more the sharp waves of water fell on him. He was left dripping until he started shivering violently. Then he was swung forward a few feet and lowered to this knees. He pulled his hands from the unlocked handcuffs and shaded his eyes as the blindfold was removed. The sun was setting. *It can't be that late.* He glanced at his penis, which stood up stiff. He glanced at her boots directly in front of him.

"Clean them."

He bent and licked each boot ferociously. The rubbing of his penis against his thighs and stomach almost made him come.

She gripped his hair and forced his head back. "You need your hair cut again. You'll go to the barber tomorrow while I'm at a lunch meeting." She brought her other hand around and held it in front of his eyes. "This is a little something to make sure you last the entire evening." She placed the cock cage over his penis quickly.

Yvonne sat down on the floor across from her bruised and beaten slave. "You thought you were so tough. I know you've had the cane and even the whip before. Most of your other owners stopped the beatings when you didn't break after ten minutes." She leaned toward him and lowered her voice. "You're already broken to me, right?"

"Yes, Mistress," he answered quickly. His breath increased its pace. *Oh god, what's happening to me?*

"This isn't only for me either." She leaned back on her pillows. "You're going to beg me by tomorrow morning." She glanced at the slave entrance. "Bring them in!"

Two kitchen slaves entered carrying two large platters. They laid these between the two of them on the floor, then withdrew silently.

"Eat up." Yvonne picked up a roast chicken breast and tore into with her teeth. "Come on. Eat. You're going to need energy."

Jake picked up a chicken leg. Once he took one bite, he started eating everything he could get his hands on. His stomach felt like an empty pit. The only thing that slowed him down was the pain caused by reaching for the food. He whimpered when the kitchen slaves returned and collected the platters.

He was allowed to relax a few minutes when she left the room. He rose as quickly as his legs allowed when she called him into the bathroom.

"Run me a bath and brush your teeth. I'll be back in a few minutes."

He turned the water on and tested it with his elbow as he had been taught the past week. He took his toothbrush from his cup and carefully brushed his teeth. He rinsed his mouth several times. He finished just as the tub was filled to the height she liked with bubbles. He started to leave but the most beautiful female body he had ever seen blocked his way. He stepped back as it entered. "Mistress," he whispered sinking to his knees.

Yvonne walked passed him and stepped into the tub. "You will help me wash."

Jake rose and took the washcloth from her hand. He washed each part of her body except her genitals that she did herself. Then she lay back in the tub and let the water flow around her when he turned on the whirlpool.

"Hope in the shower and make sure you get completely clean."

He soaped himself up, wincing as the soap touched what he was sure had been open cuts on his back, and rinsed off twice but still she was frowning. He reached for the shampoo for the third time when her voice stopped him.

"Put that nozzle on the showerhead and give yourself an enema." She sat up in her tub when he shook his head. "You really don't want me to do it to you. Believe me."

Jake swallowed. "May I pull the opaque curtain closed, Mistress?" he asked quietly.

"Please do. And make sure you soap down and rinse off afterwards," she added.

He placed the nozzle on the showerhead and removed it from its post. He clinched his teeth as he did to himself what they had done to him in jail before and after sentencing to check him for drugs.

Yvonne smiled as she heard his soft weeping. She got out of the tub and wrapped herself in a towel. "Come to the bedroom when you are done," she ordered leaving the bathroom as she heard him starting to expel his waste.

Jake returned to the main room ten minutes later. He saw her sitting on her bed in a red negligée. He swallowed in fear when she motioned for him to approach. *Damn it! Don't do that!* he cursed his cock as it pushed against its bonds. He held out his hands as she held up a pair of leather wrist cuffs.

"Kneel down and lay your upper body across the bed, arms straight."

The cuffs were strapped to ring on the other side of the bed. She stepped from the bed. Her feet kicked his legs wide. She strapped his thighs to the bed frame. He screamed as she shoved something up inside his asshole. This device was attached with straps to the cock cage in front.

Yvonne threw a blanket over him and climbed back into bed. "You can come in now," she called. From the dark of the room another female figure emerged.

General Corriger! He'd met her during his time here and she had been the woman with his mistress when he first met her. Jake watched this woman slip out of her robe and climb into bed naked. He couldn't see what they were doing but their moans caused him to strain against the bed.

Jake woke up when he felt his arms relax. He looked up to see the cuffs removed. She climbed over the bed toward him and lifted his head up. "Drink this," she said putting a glass of water to his lips. He pushed himself up by his arms to drink but found his thighs still strapped to the bed frame restricted his movement.

She took the glass and set it somewhere out of his sight. She stood on the bed and shed her negligée. "Now it's your turn to make me happy," she lowered herself so her crotch was directly in front of his face. "You couldn't help but hear how happy I was last night." Yvonne spread her legs. "See if you can do better and you'll get two questions tonight."

Jake thought for a moment. *It's been five years seen I've made love to a woman but not like this. What does she want me to do?* Just then she gripped his hair and forced his face toward what he recalled was a clitoris. *OK.* He flicked out his tongue and was rewarded with a small thrust from her hips.

His tongue slowly licked along each side of her labia, his mind latched on to the terms he'd learned in that sex ed class back in junior high, the one interesting class he'd had in school. He quickened his pace gradually until she started to rock. He placed his hands on her hips and pulled her closer. He worked his tongue down to the edge of her vagina. He stuck it in quickly.

"No," she said sharply.

He moved his tongue back up her inner lips. Slowly. Quickly. Slowly. Quickly.

"Yes!" she ordered pulling him so close he couldn't breathe.

He licked faster and faster. His hands slipped from her hips and clenched the bed sheets. He bucked against the bed. Just as he thought he would pass-out she shuddered and thrust him from her.

He tried to slow his breathing. He glanced at her. She too was trying to slow her breath.

"Not too bad," she said getting off the bed. She unstrapped his thighs. "Do you want to get off?"

"Yes," he said. He fell on the floor from her fist. "Yes, Mistress. Please."

"Follow me." She led him to the bathroom and had him kneel in the tub. She handcuffs his hands over his head to a bar and hoisted them tight. "Do you want to get off?"

Jake remembered what she had said before the evening started. "Yes, Mistress," he begged. "Please let your slave come, Mistress."

She smiled and loosened the cock cage. "You only come when I say to." She reached behind him.

Jake's eyes widened as he felt his ass vibrate. After a few seconds he started thrusting. "Oh, oh, please." He closed his eyes and concentrated on her voice. *Wait, wait for her!* The vibrating lessened and he took a breath only to feel it increase again. "Aaahhh..."

"Come," Yvonne whispered. She laughed as he shot his load over the entire wall. She removed the butt plug and the cock cage. "Take a shower and come out to eat." She washed her hands, put on her robe and left.

Jake showered quickly. He looked in the mirror and noticed another bruise forming on his face. He walked out to her bedroom and found her eating breakfast.

"Sit down and eat. You're probably very hungry. I know I am," she smiled, the first truly warm smile he had seen on her. He knelt slowly, wincing from the pain. "You'll get used to it," she said and tossed him a roll.

Jake stopped his laps when he saw her limo drive up the road to the palace. He thought about running to meet her then decided to finish his last two laps.

After the three miles, he headed back to the stables. There he took a quick shower to wash the sweat from him before he met her. He glanced in the mirror and nodded at how much he thought his body had improved in the three weeks she had been gone. *I can handle more tonight.*

Jake hurried through the slave tunnels to her bedroom. Finding it dark and empty he opened the curtains slightly. He went to the bathroom and ran a hot bubble bath. He opened the closet with the torture instruments and picked out a two inches leather collar. This he fastened around his neck along with the two matching wrist cuffs. He glanced in the bathroom mirror when he turned off the water. *I hope this isn't too forward.* He heard the lower level door open.

Yvonne stomped upstairs. Though she was mildly surprised when she found her slave prostrated a few feet from the stairs, Yvonne stepped over him to throw her pack on the bed. She ignored him and went to the bathroom. After a few minutes she walked out to the bedroom and stood at his head. "Did you run that bath for me?"

"Yes, Mistress," he answered but remained prostrate. He braced his body on his arms as his hair was grabbed and his head forced up. He tried to look past her naked body.

Yvonne bent and run her finger along the leather collar. She nodded slightly as she noticed the cuffs. "You want it, don't you, slave?"

"Yes, Mistress. Please," he heard himself whisper. His arms caught him as she let go of his hair.

"Help me with my bath," she ordered as she turned on her heel.

Jake jumped to his feet and followed her. He kept his face blank as he assisted her into the water. "Is the bath to your liking, Mistress."

"It will do," she replied. She looked at him for a moment. "Remove all your clothes." She lay back in the water and bubbles watching him disrobe. "How many miles do you do now?"

"Three, Mistress," he replied laying the last of his clothing on the floor in a neat pile. He could feel the leather more clearly now that they were his only coverings. He caught the sponge that she tossed him.

"Wash me," she ordered holding out a leg. She watched him dispassionately as he washed each limb, her neck, face, hair and back.

She took the sponge from him before he even thought of touching more of her body. "Call the kitchen and order some food. Tell them I'm in the bath and they'll know what to send up. When it gets here, bring it in."

Jake waited impatiently for the tray of food. "Thanks so much for hurrying," he snapped when the slave door opened and one of the kitchen hands entered. "I'll take care of this. Don't come back until we call you," he added as the boy left.

He found his mistress in the same position he had left her, relaxing in the now fading bubbles. He laid the tray on a small stand and moved it to the tub.

"Are you hungry, slave?"

"No, mistress. Not yet," he replied uncovering the tray to revealed meats, cheeses, breads, and various fruits.

"Good. There are some hooks in the shower. Slip the rings on the cuffs over them. Facing away from me." She took a bunch of grapes as she watched him slip the cuff rings over the hooks placed at the opposite ends of the shower so his arms were spread away from his body. Taking a remote control unit from underneath her head she pressed the button that made the hooks close.

Jake tried the hooks and found them to be strong. He glanced over his shoulders in fear and hope only to see her eating grapes in the tub.

"Tell me how you spent these three weeks," she ordered reaching for some cheese.

"I, Jake, did as you commanded, Mistress. Each morning at sun-up Jake rose, dressed and broke fast in the kitchen. Then Jake asked the steward for work. Sometimes he had chores, sometimes he didn't. If there were chores, Jake did them but if not then Jake wandered around the palace." He paused when her chewing stopped. He felt her stare on him. "Jake thought that learning about the palace would enable me, him, to obey you more quickly." He sighed in relief and she murmured her agreement and resumed eating. "After a noon meal, Jake went to the stable to run laps. After that Jake went to the library to read the books you sat aside for him," he felt his penis rise as his mind touched on the books.

"You enjoyed those books."

He wondered whether it was a question or statement but decided to answer any way. "Yes, Mistress."

"I'm only here for this evening then I'm off again. The next time I return, I hope you will be ready to accompany me on my station tour."

Yvonne stood up and exited the tub. She wrapped a towel around her and pulled the plug to let the water out. Closing the shower curtain with one hand, she turned the water on lukewarm and pointed it so it hit his body.

She left the bathroom and went to her torture closet. She dropped the towel and picked out the leather vest, chaps, gloves and a small bag. She placed the clothing on then, smiling, she returned to the bathroom. She turned off the water and released the hooks all by remote which she placed on the chaps' belt. "Come out to the bedroom."

Jake slipped his cuff rings from the hooks and stumbled from the shower wet and shivering. He went to the bedroom and stopped dead went he saw her. Quickly he lowered his eyes which now saw his penis rising again.

"On you hands and knees, slave!"

He assumed the position and felt her standing behind him. He opened his mouth as she placed the bit in front of his lips. The reins rested over his shoulders. *She's gonna ride me.* He tried not to fight knowing it would be pointless. *You want this. Don't fight her. You really liked those pictures and the last night she was here. You're hers, go with it and you'll get to come.*

"Good, you're not fighting," she whispered. She knelt behind him and forced his legs slightly apart with her own. She took a tube from the bag and squeezed the jelly into his anus. "You are my slave," she whispered slapping his buttocks. She took the strap-on dildo from the bag and fastened it around her waist. "The guards told me you liked them a lot but you don't get them any more, only me."

Jake whimpered and tried to move but found the bit pulled back tightly. He closed his eyes and tried to relax as he felt his ass being penetrated slowly. Once it was in so deep he felt as he would explode, she stopped pushing. He let out a breath through his teeth as she slowly pulled it out, stopping before it left him completely. Slowly back in and out. This continued just as slowly until he had counted thirty. He felt now a very pleasant pressure in him and found the bit loosed enough for him to glance down between his legs. His penis stood horizontal to the floor.

"Very good," Yvonne complimented him and patted his back gently. Suddenly she slapped his right butt cheek and pulled it out all the way.

Jake bucked as she slapped him again and pushed it in quickly. As he struggled, his head was forced back tightly. Slowly he tried to relax as she pumped in and out rapidly. The pressure in him rose and a sweat broke on his skin. After a while his hands slipped so he landed on his forearms. She accommodated this new angle by loosening the bit and rose up on her knees.

"Ahhh, oohh," he moaned through the bit as he felt his penis strain. Then she exited. He found the reins resting on his back and looked up at her. "Please, Mistress," he begged. He found himself filled but this time with something longer so it just touched his prostrate gland. He pushed back but found nothing there.

Yvonne lifted his head by his hair, taking the bit from him. She lay on her back and spread her legs. "Bring me to orgasm and maybe you'll come before I leave again."

"Tongue and fingers, Mistress?" he asked sliding lower to the floor so her folds were at eye level.

"Just the tongue, slave."

Jake just touched her outer lips licking all around them. Slowly he licked inward in circles to the inner lips and down her shaft. When he reached the vagina he could taste her juice but he wisely remembered she disliked any penetration. He returned to the outer lips and licked a little faster. He wanted to repeat the cycle more and more quickly but could feel his own need pressing on him for release. He returned to her shaft and licked at an increasing pace. Soon her thighs clamped over his head and she started to moan her pleasure. Encouraged he increased his pace until she was bucking into his tongue and shuddered. He licked her clean without command while her breath returned to normal. He kissed her inner right thigh. "Please, Mistress," he begged.

Suddenly his ass started to vibrate softly then more strongly. He moaned and tried to rub himself on the floor but found her hands holding the leather collar he wore preventing him from laying fully on the ground. After several minutes he felt the device stab his gland and his penis explode in pleasure.

"Clean it up then take another shower," she commanded as she removed the plug.

Jake started to rise but found her foot on his head.

"Use your tongue, slave. Hurry before it dries."

Jake felt a comment rising in his throat but shoved it down as he licked up his ejaculate slowly.

Jake went to do his laps near the stables. He had awaken to find the cuffs, collar and mistress gone that morning at sunrise. He took a few breaths before beginning the run. As he turned the first curve of the track, he thought about what he had been through since arriving there. Weeks without seeing her, then hours of torture or simply following her around. *Is she doing this on purpose? Yeah, that's it. She's trying to break my will.* With that realization he sped off to finish five miles without a thought.

"You were running from the devil out there," Mike the stable lad stated as Jake stumbled into the stable and fell onto the floor. "Bad move 'cause I've got a job for you."

"Fuck you," Jake managed to say as he gasped for air.

"The princess' orders. I'm supposed to teach you how to care for her gear and horse." Mike stood above the gasping man. "As soon as you get your breath, we'll start."

Jake focused on slowly his breath. Propping himself up on his elbows, he looked up at the ceiling. He remembered putting on the collar and cuffs before he had even seen her and dug his fingernails into the dirt. *That's not going to happen again.* He stood up and headed for the hay bin with a frown. "So what am I supposed to do with her stuff?" he demanded when he found the stable hand shoveling hay from one pile to another.

"First you learn to pitch the hay," Mike stopped and handed the pitchfork to him.

"What does this have to do with her stuff?"

"Horses eat hay whenever it's available so you have to learn how to care for it. It's really easy."

"No, no, no." Jake threw the pitchfork on the ground. "You said that she wanted me to learn to care for her gear and the horse so I ain't doing your work for you," he said and turned to leave.

"You will do whatever Mike tells you to do." Jake founded himself face to face with the chief groom. "Pick up the pitchfork and do your work."

"Whose gonna make me?" Jake stood as straight as he could and folded his hands into fists.

The chief groom stepped aside with a wave of his hand. "I'm not going to make you do anything. We're all slaves here. We should obey orders but if you don't want to, I'll just have to tell her about it."

Jake felt his stomach tighten. "Just because you don't like to do your own chores, right?"

"No. Because she'll ask me what you did when she gets back just like she did yesterday."

Jake's face turned white.

"Oh, I see," the chief groom chuckled. "You think you've earned her trust. Why would she trust a drug dealer?"

Jake's face now turned red when he groom spoke the truth. He picked the pitchfork. "Show me what to do," he said to the stable hand.

How long is she going to be gone? Jake pulled on some clean clothes. He now ate the sandwich he had picked up in the kitchen before returning to her suite to shower. No one objected to him showering there instead of the stable so since he slept on the cot next to her bed he thought it would save time. *Save time for what?* he asked himself as he walked down the spiral stairs. There on the one chair were the books he was supposed to be reading. Confident he could ignore them for the third day in a row he sat in the chair next to them and ate his sandwich. His eyes glanced at the title of the top book Sam's Submission. *Why would I be interested in that?*

He finished the sandwich and sat silently for a moment. "I'm not gonna to read it!" he announced to the room as he stood and went to the windows. He watched the sun set and when the last rays disappeared felt a tug at his heart. He turned back to the chair. Flipping on the light, he sat and opened the top book. He read until the sun rose.

Jake looked out of the lower level windows. *Ten days. God, I wish I had a watch.* He went to her desk and looked at it. He ran his hand over the top and closed his eyes. He pictured his mistress standing over him. Her shoulder length, scarlet hair tossed over one shoulder. A black leather teddy on her body and thigh high leather boots one of which she placed on his knee. He imagined himself touching that boot then opened his eyes.

Jake hurried to the books left for him, only one of the three left. He picked it up and ran his hand over the cover <u>Taken or Given: Twelve Short Erotic Tales</u>. He opened it eagerly and sat on the floor to read under the floor lamp. The first two books had aroused him against his will but now he did not fight arousal as he read.

Jake had unbuttoned his shirt and was leaning against the desk as he neared the end of the third story. He didn't hear the door open.

"You are to come with me!" the steward's voice caused Jake to throw the book in the air from fright.

"Shit! Don't do that you fuckhead!" Jake exclaimed scrabbling to his feet. At the steward's frown he remembered his buttons. "It's hot in here."

"Of course," the steward replied with a sneer. "There is a bag packed for you in that closet," the steward stated pointing to the coat closet. "Get it and follow me."

"Why?" Jake asked as he tucked in his shirt.

"She just sent orders for you to be brought to her." The steward walked to the open door. "Are you coming?"

Jake nodded and hurried to the closet. He grabbed the large khaki canvas bag and lugged it to his shoulder. "What's in this?"

"I don't know, I didn't pack it." The steward led him from the room then locked the door to the princess' suite. "I'm to take you to the doctors first before you leave."

"Why?" Jake grabbed the book and stuffed it in the bag.

"She didn't tell me," the steward answered.

They took the main stairways down to the clinic. After knocking they entered. "You know what to do?" the steward asked the two doctors.

"Yes, we just received the letter," the man answered taking the bag from Jake. "You can wait out here for him," he told the steward.

"Come with us," the female doctor told Jake.

Jake followed them into the room where he had been examined months ago. "Another physical?"

"We'll start with that," the female doctor said taking the letter from her partner.

Jake stripped and did as he was told. When told he was in better health he smiled. "I'd better be after running those laps every day."

The female doctor took something large and black from the bag he had brought. The male doctor held it up and straightened all the straps of black leather.

"What's that?" Jake asked though he knew from the books what it was.

"You're to wear what we put on you until you reach the princess' camp and are told to remove them." The man motioned for Jake to step down from the exam table.

Jake didn't struggle as the straps fit over his shoulders. He saw the woman hand the man several small locks. Straps were fastened around his upper arms and thighs. The three straps in back were tightened and locked. Next a collar, wider than his permanent one was locked around his neck. He couldn't move his head now so just watched the items as they were handed to the man and felt them lock on him. First cuffs were locked on his wrists.

"Wait," the woman said. "We should drain him before doing the rest."

The man nodded and helped Jake lie back on the exam table. Jake felt his arms and legs restrained.

"No!" he screamed as he felt his ass and urethra invaded. He continued screaming as he felt water pumping into his ass and being sucked from his bladder. Then the water was sucked for his ass. He kept screaming until he didn't feel any more pain. He opened his eyes to find the woman looking down at him with a frown.

"That was for your own good, idiot," she said angrily. She nodded to her partner who silently spread Jake's ass cheeks.

Jake clenched his teeth as something large was pushed into him. Then he felt strapped pulled around his semi-erect cock. He heard the click of two more locks then both doctors lifted him to his feet.

He put clothes on as commanded, the leather harness and chastity devices were hidden but he still felt them and squirmed. The man helped him put on his socks and shoes. "You'll get used to it on the journey," he assured him.

"Do you know why I have to wear this?" Jake asked. He felt shame creep over him as the man stood up to face him.

"So you don't misbehave or get used before you reach her."

"She's the only one with the keys," the woman added. She opened the door to the waiting room. "You can leave now. The steward will show the way."

Jake followed the steward to the stables. He noticed the steward seemed amused but bit his tongue before saying anything. *He knows. Everyone knows.* Jake looked at the wagon that he was led to. "I go in there?"

"Yes, the guards will take you to the princess." The steward threw the bag into the wagon and watched with a smile as Jake struggled inside. As the wagon pulled away from the palace, the steward chuckled to himself.

Jake drank the shake that the female guard had given him. *No solid foods until we reach the camp* he thought bitterly. He watched the male guard closely. *Do I know him.* After the guards finished eating this guard came to him unbuttoning his pants. Jake tried to stand but was stopped when on his knees. "Don't try it!" he spat at the guard.

The female guard stood behind the male guard. "He's got a chastity device on. You might as well leave him alone."

"I had him that way before." Jake froze as he recognize one of his rapists. "I'll have him another way now."

Jake fought back as the man tried to force his head down. He relaxed when the guard released his grip only to find himself tackled onto his back and the guard straddling his head.

"Hey hold his feet and I'll help you get some action too," the man said. Jake felt his kicking feet grabbed and held to the floor. "Open it!"

Jake clenched his teeth and shook his head. He tried not to give in when his nose was closed but finally had to gasp for breath. He felt the huge cock forced into his mouth. In rage he closed his teeth.

"Bastard!" the guard screaming pulled out and hit him on the jaw. He grabbed the slave's head and held the nose again. "Do it nice or I'll kill you here and now!"

Jake gasped for breath and felt the cock shoved deeper into his throat. He didn't bite but struggled for breath.

"Just open your throat and let me do it so you can breath through your nose!" the guard ordered.

In Jake's mind some of the pictures from the books flash before his eyes. He tried to relax. *Just let them do it and get it over. You'll be there tomorrow.* Telling himself this seemed to relax his throat and he felt his breath flowing from his nostrils. He started counting the thrusts. *Five, six, seven.* He struggled again when the warm slimy come started filling his throat. The guard got up after a final thrust and rolled him over. Jake threw up.

He felt something kick his feet. "I don't' want him after that!" he heard the woman complain.

"I'll rinse his mouth out for you," the man said.

Jake felt himself pulled away from that area to a more grassy one. The woman pushed him into a sitting position. "You bite me and I'll rip your head off!" she promised. The man gave him something medicine tasting to rinse his mouth with several times. Jake even managed to gargle and get some of the filth from his throat.

Jake lay back down on the woman's lap. "Your turn," he snipped at her. She let his head fall as she stood up. She removed her pants and underwear then straddled his face. Before she said anything, he licked her already wet and swollen clit.

"Hey! He must like you," the man said squatting down to watch.

Jake continued to lick and suck at his own pace even after the woman grabbed his hair and tried to force him to go faster. *No. I do it my way.* He brought her to the edge of orgasm and started to back off when she stood up.

"Get it out!" he heard her order. Jake managed to sit up and watch as the man took down his pants and grabbed her. He watched in anger as they fucked in front of him. Jake wiped the dying juices from his face on his sleeve. They didn't notice that he had returned to the wagon until the next morning.

Jake blinked in the afternoon sun as he was jerked from the wagon by the two guards. His eyes focused clearly and saw the too familiar figure in black fatigues. He pulled his arms free and prostrated himself as she approached. Her black boots stopped in front of his face.

"Stand up!" her voice sounded strange. Yvonne grabbed his hair and forced his head up for her to view. "Open your mouth!" She looked inside and saw a red rash and bruises. Yvonne released him and pointed to the large tent from which she had come. "Go in and wait for me." She pushed past him and went to the guards. "Corriger!"

Jake paused once he was near the tent. He watched the general join his mistress. "Yes," he whispered when the male guard was thrown to the ground by the princess' blow. He went into the tent with a smile.

"No one touches my property without my permission! General Corriger!" Yvonne yelled loud enough for everyone in camp to hear.

"Yes, your majesty." Valerie glared down at the guard in anger.

"She used him too!" the male guard stated pointing to his partner.

Yvonne turned to the woman. "Is that true?"

"I told him not too..."

"Is that true?"

The woman turned deathly white under her liege lady's cruel gaze. "Yes."

"Execute both of them," she ordered just loud enough for those nearby to here.

"Are you sure?" the General asked with a glance at the two guards. "You don't want a trial?"

Yvonne looked at the soldiers gathered around her. "Did you hear them confess?"

"Yes!" the soldiers answered almost in unison.

"I believe the law says that I am within my rights, General."

"Your sentence will be carried out." The general watched her liege lady return to her tent then turned to the two condemned guards. "How could you be so stupid?"

"You said you wanted him scared..." the man began.

"But not touched!" The general glanced around and signaled for two soldiers. "I'll try to make it quick," she whispered.

Yvonne stormed into her tent. She walked past the prostrate slave and poured two goblets of wine. "Stand up and drink this," she said.

Jake rose slowly and took the goblet. "Thank you, Mistress."

She watched him silently while they finished drinking. "They forced you?" she asked taking the goblet from him.

"Yes, Mistress," he answered, eyes respectfully focused over her shoulder.

"Are you lying to me?"

Jake focused his eyes on hers. "No, Mistress." After the answer he returned his eyes to the empty space above her shoulder.

"Take your clothes off and close your eyes."

Jake quickly did as he was bid. As he stood motionlessly, he heard the locks unclick.

"Open your eyes. Behind that curtain is the bathroom. Go in there, get clean, and put on the clothes you find there before returning here for supper."

Jake bowed and went behind the curtain. He slipped out of the straps. The butt plug hurt as he removed it. He washed the leather and plastic off with a cleaner sitting on a small table. He then took a quick but thorough shower using the nozzle for an enema and the razor to shave his body. Stepping out of the shower, he heard voices in the tent. He glanced out of the curtain and saw the general standing and speaking seriously to the princess.

He returned to a chair that had his clothes folded over them.

50

Nice stuff. I wonder what she wants. He put on the silk underpants, cotton pants and silk shirt. The pair of sandals with matching brown vest finished the outfit. He looked at the mirror set up in the room. The blue pants and white shirt were clearly rich material. *I guess I better go find out.*

When Jake entered the main area of the tent he found his mistress alone. She was facing away from him so he softly cleared his throat.

Yvonne spun around. "Very nice. I hope you feel comfortable in them."

"Yes, thank you, Mistress." Jake waited for a few seconds before approaching her. "May your slave do anything for you, Mistress."

"Yes. Guard!" One of the two guards at the opening of her tent entered. "Take my slave to the cook and then bring him back with my meal. He'll learn the way after this."

Jake bowed and followed the guard out. These were soldiers, not the palace guards who had raped him, so he tried to relax and memorize the path. They led him several yards away to another large tent, this one had all the flaps open and delicious scents drifted out.

Jake nodded at the cook when he was introduced.

"Are you allergic to any foods or preservatives?" the large man asked wiping his hands on his apron.

"Not that I know of," Jake replied with a smile.

The cook nodded. "Good because the baskets are ready to go." Two youths handed Jake two large baskets. "You can carry those can't you?" the cook asked as the slave struggled to grip them.

"I got them." Jake looked around at the kitchen help and noticed they all wore uniforms very similar to the guards who had brought him here. "You're not slaves?" he blurted out.

The kitchen staff laughed. "No. Everyone here is free," the cook replied with a grin. "Except for you and any captives we might pick up along the way."

Jake felt his face turn red. He turned on his heel and hurried as fast as the baskets allowed from the tent. The guards soon caught up with him. *I hate them all.* "I can carry it!" he snapped when one of them tried to take one of the baskets. "I'm the slave aren't I?"

"Hey, I don't care," the guard replied.

They hurried back to the tent. Jake went inside as soon as they started to part the tent flaps.

"Did you learn the way?" Yvonne asked not looking up from the papers she was reading.

Jake glanced angrily at the guards. "Yes, Mistress," his voice did not betray his anger. "Get out!" he mouthed at the guards who left with a shrug.

As he went to the large table in the room to set the baskets on it, his head was snapped by her slap. He dropped the baskets on the table and sank to his knees, head on the floor in front of her boots.

"You have a problem with my soldiers?"

"No, Mistress," he said then found his head forced up by his hair.

"I know everything that happens in this camp and in my palace. I'll ask the question once more. You have a problem with my soldiers?"

Jake felt his face drain of all its color. "Yes, Mistress." As soon as he said it, she released his hair.

"What's the problem?"

Jake looked up at her to find her just sitting on the edge of the table. He sat back on his heels and focused his eyes over her shoulder. "Jake thought the kitchen staff would be slaves too. Jake just didn't know he was your only one here. Mistress."

"This is an army. We work through mutual respect and need. I wouldn't have brought you except you can take care of my little needs so that more troops are free to fight and live their own lives. She got off the table and sat in the chair. "Serve the food."

Jake slowly stood up. He glanced at her as he unpacked the baskets. One had the plates, silverware, napkins, goblets and a bottle of wine. The other held the food in various containers. As he dished out the food onto her plate and poured the wine he almost spoke a couple of times.

"You have a daily question so ask it now if you want," she reminded him as she started eating. "Don't waste it. The other plate is for you so eat up."

Jake muttered "Thank you, Mistress," then filled his own plate.

There were three other chairs but he remained standing to eat so he could serve her. After he refilled her goblet, he spoke. "They said that you pick up slaves on your missions."

Yvonne frowned slightly. "Is that a question?"

"No, Mistress," he explained quickly. "Aren't criminals the only slaves?"

"That's your question?"

"Yes, Mistress."

Yvonne set her goblet down. "Well, our citizens can only be enslaved for crimes. But our enemies aren't' protected by our laws. I don't enslave enemies often. Usually I just ransom them back to their relatives, good relations with people I may soon rule. Or I have them executed." She sipped her wine again and looked him over. "Of course, if you stop pleasing me then I might just choose someone new."

Jake set his chicken leg down and looked at her. "What would happen then?"

"You only have one question per day," Yvonne reminded him with a cold smile. "Use your imagination and finish your food."

Jake entered the tent and bowed after returning from the mess tent. He waited for her invitation before kneeling next to her chair where she set reading. He stayed there when she stood up and went to the bathroom. She returned tossing him the book he had packed with him.

"You're not finished." Yvonne sat down in her chair and picked up the field reports. "Read one story then stop."

"Mistress?"

"Yes."

"Jake was at the end of one story when he was called away. May he finish it and read another?" He braced himself for a kick or blow for asking another question.

"No, just finish that one."

Jake waited but no punishment came. He opened the book and tried to read the last three pages slowly. His pulse was racing and his skin was just covered with perspiration by the time he read the last word. He glanced at her chair then jumped to his feet. *Where is she?*

He went to the entrance and stuck his head through the tent flaps. "Has her majesty left the tent?" he asked the two new guards.

When they silently shook their head, he hurried back to the center of the tent. *Oh, shit! Damn it!* He almost fainted when she emerged from the bathroom in khaki pajamas. "Forgive me," he begged crawling to her feet as quickly as he could.

"Did you enjoy the story?" she replied with a slight grin.

"Yes, Mistress," he looked eagerly up over her shoulder, bracing himself for a beating or the feel of leather on his skin. His heart sank when she simply walked passed him empty handed.

"Take your clothes off and lay them on one of the chairs," she ordered flatly.

Jake scrambled to his feet and faced her, his hope returning when he saw her sitting on the top of her bed. He removed and laid aside his clothes as soon as possible.

"There a black case in the bathroom on the table. After you've used the toilet, brushed your teeth and washed up, bring it to me."

Jake hurried and prepared for the evening. He combed his hair neatly and smiled at himself in the mirror when he noticed how large his cock already was. He touched the black case but decided not to open it.

Yvonne took the case from her slave and told him spread his legs and close his eyes. She fastened the chastity device on him again but not the butt plug. "Open your eyes. You sleep at the foot of my bed. There's a blanket for you."

Jake opened his mouth in surprise when she crawled under the covers and turned the light out. In the darkness he was tempted to touch her. *Damn! This is the punishment for what those bastards did!* He felt his way to the end of her bed, found the blanket and curled up on the rug.

He pulled the blanket around him trying to block out his thoughts. Scenes from the story kept invading his mind. Soon these merged with the experiences he had suffered under her hand. He tried to awaken but found himself further and further into the dreams.

Yvonne sat in bed smiling into the dark as his moans increased in volume and desire. She placed one finger to her lips to keep from laughing as she praised the doctor's for supplying her with the tranquilizer lotion she had spread on the chastity cage.

Two weeks! Jake sat the breakfast basket on the table in the mess kitchen. *How long is this punishment going to last? What can I do to make her touch me? Even her fist against my jaw would get me off.* He touched his caged cock absently then hurried from the tent.

"Watch where you're going slave!"

Jake looked into the hate-filled eyes of General Corriger. He smiled. "I'm sorry, General. I'm just so tired from last night I must have dozed off while walking," he lied with ease. "I'll try to be more careful where I walk."

Corriger grabbed his silk collar and pulled him to his toes. "Keep your eyes open slave!" She released him with a push that almost made him fall.

"Bitch," he whispered as she stormed away. *At least she ain't getting any either.* He straightened his shirt and returned to the tent.

Yvonne threw a bit and reins at him. "Saddle my horse!"

Jake caught the bit and reins. "My question from last night. Are we leaving, Mistress?"

"I'm leaving on a raid with my best soldiers. Now go saddle my horse."

"Yes, Mistress." Jake hurried to the stable where he found her black mare eagerly pacing her stall. He brushed the horse down and saddled her as he had been shown back at the palace. Just as he led the horse outside, the reins were taken from his hands.

Yvonne strapped her saddlebags on the mare quickly then mounted. "Pick up your meals like always. There's a new book for you on the table in my tent. Read as much as you like," she added with a smiled.

Jake watched her gallop away. After he could no longer see her, he returned to the tent. There he found a leather book without a title sitting on the table. He picked it up and opened to the table of contents. *Introduction. Ted. Brian. Roger. Bill. Scott. Neal. Dean. Alex. Zach. Trent. Lyle.* He set the book back on the table. *Later.* He went to collect the laundry to take to the camp cleaners.

Jake gripped the book with both hands as he finished *Roger*. It had been four nights since she had left and he had read one section of the book each night. *I want to go there,* he thought about the school described in the book.

After four nights of reading, he found himself now opening the bag he had brought with him. He looked at the mirror in the bathroom as he placed the collar around his neck. *I wish the metal one was off so I could feel it better.* Next he put the wrist cuffs on. Unable to fasten the straps behind his back, he put the body harness back in the bag.

Next he took out a set of nipple clamps and snapped them on slowly. "Ooohhh..." he moaned as they burned him. After a few minutes the pain dulled. He looked in the mirror and noticed his cock turning a dark red as it pushed helpless against the cage.

He took out a thin but long butt plug. His hands trembled as he smeared it with lube. Then he bent down at the knees and spread his legs. He closed his eyes as he pushed it into himself. As he slammed it in and out faster and faster he heard himself crying out, "Mistress. Please. Please." Finally the plug touched his prostrate and he felt sudden release and pain as his cock pulsed against the leather straps.

After regaining his footing and his breath, he removed the plug and stumbled to the sink to clean it off. He noticed his penis was still enlarged but didn't hurt as much. He didn't know what happened but he felt a little better as he went to sleep at the foot of her bed.

"Oops!"

Jake glared up at the General as he picked up the remains of his breakfast that she had knocked to the ground for the sixth day in a row.

"I'm just so clumsy," Corriger said, kicking him in the rib cage and knocking him on his butt. "Oops! I did it again."

"That's it!" Jake jumped to his feet. "You watch where you're going, bitch!"

"What did you call me?" Corriger smiled at the soldiers who accompanied her.

"Bitch." Jake rolled up his silk sleeves and took a fighting stance. "You're just jealous because she's chosen me over you." Jake didn't see the kicked that knocked him to the ground.

"Get him!" Corriger ordered her soldiers.

Jake fought against the two men but only found himself with a bloody nose. He let himself go limp so they had to drag him to the middle of the camp where the general waited with a mounted soldier. Jake's hands were tied together and the rope given to the mounted woman.

"Take him for a good run!" Corriger glared after the horse and the slave running after it. "Faster!" She turned as the soldiers around her took up the chant. "Faster!"

After three gallops around the entire camp, the rider returned, the slave stumbling behind her. "Look at this," Corriger clicked her tongue. "Look at these lovely clothes that she gave you and now they're ruined." She grabbed his hair and forced his head back so he had to kneel in order to breathe. "She's going to be very angry with you."

"Bitch," he spat into her eyes. He stood up shakily as she backed away from him.

"Strip him and bind him to the pole!" She ordered two of the soldiers. "Do it!" she yelled when they hesitated. "You! Go get me the biggest whip you can find! One of the horse whips!"

Corriger walked around the pole so she could glare at his face as he was tied to it face down. "You will beg me to stop. You will call me mistress too."

"Never. Jake exists for her." When the words left his lips he felt a weight fall from his body. "Do your worst, bitch!" he screamed. His head stuck the pole as she slapped him.

Jake braced for the blows. *I can take anything you got bitch.* His body arced in pain when the first strike fell. He clenched his teeth to keep from screaming. *One. Two. Three. Four. Five. Six. Seven. Eight. Nine. Bitch! Ten.* "No!" he screamed finally.

"Beg me to stop." she ordered signaling the soldier to stop the whipping.

Jake braced for the next blows. "Never!" After a few more, he was screaming wordlessly with every strike. He felt something hot and wet running down his back. *Blood.* His mind ran through his options as his screams became weaker.

"Beg me to stop, damn you!" Corriger yelled at him as the blows fell. She grabbed him by the hair and looked at him. "Call me mistress."

Jake just blinked his hate-filled eyes and bit his lip as the blows continued. Soon all he saw was darkness.

"What's going on?" Yvonne asked the scout returning from the camp. The young woman sitting behind her tightened her handcuffed hands on her captor's jacket.

"The General appears to be beating someone to death, your majesty."

Yvonne narrowed her eyes. "Come on!" she ordered her troops as she galloped into camp. Seeing the camp gathered around the whipping pole she quickly slipped the woman off her horse then dismounted throwing her the reins. The crowd grew silent as she pushed through it. Upon seeing the bloody body of her slave tied to the post, she struck the soldier handling the whip in the neck, sending him to the ground unconscious.

"What the fuck is going on here?" she demanded from the general who walked angrily around the pole.

"Yvonne," Corriger's face turned white. "Your majesty. I was just... ummm.. punishing him..."

"For what?" Yvonne walked to her frightened lover. Her elite troops ordered the other soldiers back and made a circle around their liege lady, general and the pole. "Take him down and to the medical center."

"He wouldn't obey me while you were gone, challenging my authority in camp."

"He's not your property nor is he a soldier." Yvonne turned to the soldiers glancing over the shoulders of her elite troops. "Did my property disobey any camp rules while I was gone?"

Yvonne nodded as all gathered around murmured in the negative. "He obeys me and no one else."

"He was disrespectful!"

Yvonne laughed. "I know. That's why I like him. And that's why I'm going to be lenient with you, Valerie. Ann!" The woman who had ridden behind her emerged through the crowd. "This is a present I brought back for you. Take her and go to your tent." Yvonne turned to a few of her elite troops. "Escort General Corriger to her tent and make sure she stays there until further notice."

Corriger took the woman's cuffed hands and led her away. They stopped at the sound of her name.

"Valerie. You better pray he lives."

Jake glared at the nurse as she took his temperature for the third time that day. "I feel fine!" he insisted.

"Well, we'll see when you get your tests results back." She handed him a glass of ice water. "Drink this."

"Yeah, yeah," he said taking a sip for her benefit then sitting on the table next to him. He remembered being brought back to the palace clinic a few days after the beating. How many weeks it had been he wasn't too sure. She hadn't stopped by once.

"What are you thinking about."

Jake jumped up from his bed at the sound of his mistress' voice. "About you. You came. Mistress. Please, sit down," he said motioning to the bed.

"You too. You're still weak," she said sitting on the cot next to his.

"Jake is ready for your use, Jake is ready for service, Jake exists only for you..."

"Sit down," she insisted.

"Yes, Mistress." Jake sat and couldn't tear his eyes away from her. She wore a light green dress, the first he had ever seen her in, brown boots and a wide hat. He felt his cock raise then remembered his eyes and focused them over her shoulder.

"I brought you something," she said taking a leather book from her shoulder bag. "You didn't get to finish it."

Jake took the book and moaned when he recognized it.

"You don't like it?"

"Jake is surprised to see you, Mistress. They removed his collar so," he let the possibilities linger in the air.

"That had to be removed for medical care. As was your chastity belt as I'm sure you've noticed and taken advantage of."

Jake shook his head.

"Oh, please. How many times have you gotten off since you've been here?"

Jake looked her in the eyes. "None, Mistress, not without your permission."

Yvonne smiled slightly and moved to sit next to him. "Looks like you can still do it," she said nodding at the bulge in his pajama bottoms. She reached and opened the pants to let the cock jump free. "We'll have to get you a new collar."

"Mistress," he continued as she nodded approval. "Please let Jake wear your collar again."

Yvonne moved closer to him and grabbed his hair to bring his face closer to hers. "Why?" she demanded with a pleased glance at his now purple-red cock.

"Jake doesn't exist except for you," he answered with all his being, freed from all concerns outside her voice and body.

Yvonne released him and moved away on the bed slightly. She nodded as he sat up to try to remain near her. "Come!"

Jake felt his body arc with the power of the orgasm that had been waiting for over a month. After a minute or more, he lay gasping on the bed. "Thank you, Mistress," he whispered.

"Sit up!"

Jake sat up on his knees, ignoring the still warming ejaculate that covered his stomach and groin. He smiled as she showed him the two-inch leather collar with his registration as her slave on it in gold. He stuck his neck out eagerly as she fastened it around his neck.

"Report to my suite when they release you, slave!" she ordered raising to her feet.

"Yes, Mistress," he cried tears of joy as he jumped off the bed to prostrate himself at her feet. He used his skills to observe what she did with his doctor from this position and it puzzled him.

Yvonne stopped and the two women spoke, then the princess touched the doctor's shirt collar, letting her hand slip inside slightly. The doctor's face looked paler and she nodded slightly. Then the doctor simply looked at him after the mistress left for several seconds until he sat back onto the bed.

Jake opened his mouth to talk but she simply left the room. Jake just smiled and got back into bed determined to get back up to his full health as soon as possible so he could return to the future Queen of the United Eastern States.

Justice

Drip. Plop. Drip. Plop. Drip. Plop.

He lost count around half a million and found himself falling into a pool of water. As the waves rocked and swirled, climbing his chest, splashing against his chin, Jake screamed. The cry echoed back from the darkness. There was no water around him except for that maddening drip.

The day he was released from the palace hospital was stuck in his mind. The doctor, a kind woman, had been very quiet, refusing to look at him as he was escorted from the room he had shared with other injured royal slaves into a back office. She had neither spoken to him nor looked at him since his mistress had last visited him. Then she simply gave her assistants direct instructions and they gave Jake his final exam.

At first it had seemed like he was being prepared for a meeting with his owner. He had been shaved, given an enema, his vitals signs checked, and even given a nasty health drink. He had been dressed in loose, easily removable clothing and escorted out of the hospital. The doctor had touched his arm briefly but hadn't spoken; she had just looked at him with her sad brown eyes.

He had been taken into a completely dark room and restrained with ankle and wrist cuffs. His legs and arms had been pulled until he cried out. His clothing had been removed. He had known better than to speak or to cry out when the beating began because he was certain it was his mistress reminding him of his position.

The method of beating had concerned him only in that it had been unusual for Yvonne. She liked to switch from one whip to another, intersperse the beating with threats in his ear, taking breaks for food and drink. This beating, however, had begun hard, with a leather cat of at least nine tails, each with knots at the end. The blows had come in a steady rhythm, also unlike his owner's style.

The beating had paused and he had heard a second pair of footsteps in the room. With a nervous swallow Jake had ventured to ask his question. "Mistress, why are you doing this?" There had been silence, and then the rain of blows had fallen again. The beating had continued until the lightning sting of the lashes simply disappeared. He suspected he had fallen unconscious, but no one had answered him when he demanded to know what was going on.

At first he had tried to count the days as they passed in total darkness. He had based his count on the assumption of one meal per day, which he had figured was all this punishment would allow. It had to be a punishment; the alternative was unthinkable, impossible, and his mind had almost forgotten her earlier statement of what the Palace did to unwanted slaves.

Those first few days he had asked the unseen owner of the hands that fed him what he had done wrong. Pressing the question over and over had confirmed a fear. His mistress was not the one feeding him, for she would have hit him, or at least reminded him firmly that only one question was allowed each day. So he had then asked who he had been given to, since there was no reported crime that he was here for. That question had only been met with laughter, laughter far away, perhaps three yards, and yet clearly the Princess Yvonne's voice.

Jake now bit his cheek. The shackles on his hands, stretched out to his sides, made it impossible to plug his ears. So now he tried to hurt himself in any way he could to pull his mind away from the sound and the answer he was searching for but which alluded him. The royal family never sold slaves. Yvonne had told him she wouldn't give him away. That left one alternative only, and it was too horrible to think of even though he would have gladly accepted it just 32 days after he arrived at the Palace.

The water stopped just as he burst into tears moments later. And Jake then quieted himself and listened carefully. No, there was not even a tiny remnant of the sound. He swung his head back into the air. Except for his feet on the cold stone floor and the metal on his ankles and wrists he wasn't in contact with anything other than the air.

The hair on the back of his neck rose as he heard footsteps approaching. This would be food, at least, and a chance to try and get answers. He jerked back when something touched his face, tickling the beard that was growing now after at least two weeks by his feeble calculations. Her laughter hit his ears. "Mistress, please," he muttered as he reached out with his dry tongue, trying to touch her.

"Ah, still trying to please me?" Yvonne asked.

"Yes, Mistress, Jake is trying to please you. Please tell your slave what to do?" he begged and choked slightly on a cry in his throat.

"You enjoy pleasing me, don't you, Jake?"

Jake opened his eyes and could barely make out a human figure against the darkness. "Yes, Mistress. It is your slave's existence."

"But you enjoy it a great deal. Correct?" Yvonne's voice had a dangerous edge to it.

"Yes, Mistress," Jake simply replied. He licked his lips as she laughed again.

"And that is the problem," Yvonne began. "You see, drug dealer, you're supposed to be punished, not having a holiday. I guess enslavement just isn't appropriate for you."

Jake's mouth fell open as he heard the words and the thoughts in his head, the ones he had until now so successfully ignored He called after the retreating footsteps, "Mistress! Please, Mistress! Please, come back! Please!" His crying died down as he heard the door shut.

There was no food after this. No water dripping either. Nothing to help him count the time. Just the torment in knowing she was starving him to death.

Try as he might, he just couldn't accept it; it just made no sense. The princess was cruel but fair. Yvonne was strong but beautiful. He had been blessed with her smile on a few occasions. She had even fired her lover in his defense. She cared for him; he had been so certain.

In later moments he would remember that she was called the Butcher for a reason. After that moment he gave up hope of even seeing the world beyond the dungeon. Weeping, spending the last energy he had, he prayed that God, whatever that was, would forgive him.

Jake blinked his eyes as best he could as he vaguely felt his body being lifted. His arms and legs were numb, and yet he knew they had been uncuffed. His head throbbed loudly as it swung. A look into the darkness showed the dungeon upside down as he was moved.

"Fuck! He's still not light." A hauntingly familiar voice reached through his pain and hunger.

"What's ... going ... on," he whispered as the dungeon receded. A door was shut behind him, and the light outside was brighter. From his position over the shoulder of this new tormentor he could see military-style boots. Perhaps he had assumed too quickly that death would come easily in the confines of the dank prison.

A scent was the first signal Jake's brain registered. It was a warm, soft scent like flowers in the woods under the sunlight after a gentle rain or at least what he thought heaven might smell like. "Thank you," he whispered to God.

"You're welcome," a woman's voice answered.

Jake opened his eyes slowly and focused on the voice's owner, a woman of thin build with long brown hair wrapped into several locks by ribbons. Dressed in brown shorts, a tank top, and a slave collar around her neck she hardly represented the angel he'd been expecting. His attempt to sit up met with little success, so he sighed and just watched as his caretaker pulled up a chair and sat next to him. "Who are you?" he asked.

"Ann," the woman replied simply. "If you think you can eat something, I'll help you," she added. Her voiced had an unfamiliar accent to it.

Jake nodded slowly, then tried to sit up again. This time the angel helped him by lifting his shoulders and placing a few pillows beneath him. He looked around the room as well as his weakened state allowed. It wasn't anywhere he'd been before and was far too Spartan for the Butcher's tastes. Maybe she'd changed her mind and just given him away.

"Here is some soup with those cute tiny crackers you have," Ann said as she pulled the chair up closer. She held out a spoonful and let him eat at his own pace. "You must start slow," she added when he reached for the bowl himself.

Jake waited to ask the important questions until he had finished the soup, the tray was taken away, and he was lowered back down onto the bed. "So where am I?"

The angel blinked at him with a smile.

"Who owns me now?" he asked but received the same silence. "Look, I'm not going to cause problems; I'd just like to know what's expected of me."

Ann stood up. "To get well again." She moved the chair away and left his view.

In the background he heard a door open, shut and lock. Jake sighed, cursed himself for being in such a situation in the first place, and then cursed God for not answering his prayer.

With the Butcher it had been a punishment but also a pleasure, one ripped from him everyday, forced from his body in delightfully wicked ways. A new owner was just another inconvenience to be endured and fought against. As he yawned and felt sleep take him over, the image of a cruel face framed by shoulder-length scarlet hair filled his sight. "Mistress," he moaned into the darkness.

He spent the next five days resting, eating a increasingly complex diet, and attempting to get answers from the angel. Jake set the half-eaten wheat roll on his tray and looked directly at his nurse. "When are you going to answer my questions?"

Ann just smiled and started to take his tray.

Jake caught her hands in his and sat up so their faces were inches apart. "I want to know where I am and who is having you do all this!"

"My, my, my," a new voice interrupted. It was the same voice that he'd heard when he'd been carried from the dungeon. The sound made him release the angel and look around the room. From a poorly-lit corner a figure emerged. With her blonde hair cut much shorter than it had been during her time as the heir's chief aide, it took the slave a couple of seconds to recognize her. Corriger chuckled when realization flashed in his eyes. "Oh, yes, it's me again. Isn't this a surprise?" she mocked him as she motioned for the angel to leave.

Jake looked at Ann but didn't attempt to speak to her as she removed his lunch tray. He glared at the jealous general as he braced himself for flight if necessary and possible. "You're the last person I want to be owned by," he said flatly.

"And you're the last person I'd ever want to own," Corriger replied. "So you'll be as relieved as I when tell you that I don't own you."

"Then who? Who do you work for now?" Jake's mind filed through the images of big corporate bosses who hired personal security forces and the aristocracy he'd seen in the palace from time to time. It made sense now. Yvonne had been planning to kill him but needed to use him for political gain.

"You'll see soon enough," Corriger replied. She walked to him and looked down at him, her hands at her sides, fists clenched. "Get up!"

Jake's fear melted as the hatred he felt for this woman who had ended his life flared up. "No." The blow was expected, but still it sent him half-falling out of bed. He looked up at her and licked the blood at the corner of his mouth. "The answer is still no, bitch," he tossed out with a snort.

"Ann!" Corriger called out, and immediately the angel returned and stood next to her, her beautiful face attentively watching the woman. "Get up, boy!"

Jake shook his head, then gasped as the general grabbed the slave girl by her hair then backhanded his angel of mercy.

"Each time you disobey me, I'll punish your little nurse," Corriger stated. She yanked the slave to her feet. "Get up!"

Jake swallowed once then rose to his feet, his eyes flashing. "Leave her alone," he said, his voice low and as threatening as it could be given his position.

Corriger laughed and then bent the angel's head back and planted a big kiss on her bruised lips. The slave responded by touching the general's arms lightly, embracing her. Corriger released Ann and smiled at Jake as he made a gagging sign with his fingers pointing toward his mouth. "Ann, take him and get him cleaned up, as I explained earlier."

"Yes, Mistress," the slave girl said. She held out her hand to

Jake, who took it eagerly.

Once outside the room and into a bathroom several yards down a hall that seemed vaguely familiar in that it was large, like all homes of the rich and spoiled, Jake pushed his companion against the wall gently. "You and me, let's get out of here."

"And go where?" Ann asked with a tiny frown as she pulled free of him.

"Anywhere that isn't here. There must be a country that doesn't have good relationships with the United Eastern States," he added at the slavegirl's frown. "We'll find out who hates this place most and go there," he said. He slammed his fist into the wall as the girl just shook her head. "Look, I've run before, it can be done."

"And you've always been caught," Ann pointed out as she turned to the bathtub.

"Well, I'm a little better educated now. If you can tell me where we are and how far from the border, I can get us there," he promised.

Ann knelt down by the tub as it filled with water. "No. Now get out of those clothes and into the tub. We have a lot of work to do."

Jake sighed and agreed silently by taking off the soft sleep shirt. The truth was that he wasn't ready to run, not until he learned more of what was going on and figured out some way to make the blonde bitch Corriger pay for losing him the best thing he'd had in years. He'd been a slave, but at least it was to royalty, and he'd had more freedom there than he'd ever had in the city he'd been born in. Not that he would ever admit any of this to anyone, not even to his Mistress.

"So what did you do to be enslaved?" Jake asked once he was settled into the tub. He chuckled as the slave girl's soapy sponge tickled his sides.

"Nothing," Ann said. She dipped the sponge deeper, moving it in tight circles as she stroked his cock and thighs. She watched his face, but he only looked back at her, the organ under her hand not changing in the least. Frowning, she pulled one leg up from the water and started working on it.

Jake caught himself on the sides of the tub with his arms. "Hey, take it easy," he said. "So you were sold for a debt then?" he guessed.

"No, just captured by Yvonne the Butcher," the slave girl

stated.

Jake sat up and pulled his legs under him. "You're from another country? Damn, I knew you had an accent!" Ann nodded and moved up so she could work on his back. There was silence, then Jake inquired further. "So why haven't you been ransomed yet?"

"Who would ransom a slave? Very easily replaced where I'm from," Ann said with a guffaw.

"I don't understand," Jake said. "What kind of place are you from?"

"Someplace where they don't even pretend to have laws other than those in some old sacred book that only the Prophet is allowed to read," Ann said, and Jake sensed that there was a bit of sadness in that answer. "A place where you're born into your station in life without hope of change. I've always been a slave."

"That sounds sucky," Jake sighed. "So I suppose you like Corriger better than what you had before?" he asked.

There was a pause. "Yes. Her demands are of a more personal nature." There was a shy giggle. "I'd always been taught God would strike you with lightning for joining with another of your own sex," she admitted. "But I'm still here, and better fed and clothed than before."

Jake narrowed his eyes a bit as the angel stood up and pulled a chair to the tub. She nodded and handed him a razor. "Oh, great, I get to see what I look like," he said as she held a mirror up to him. His face was covered with dark brown and black hair, but it wasn't very long, maybe indicating only two to three weeks of growth. "I take it my new owner likes the clean-shaven look?"

"I don't really know. I've never met her," Ann answered.

Jake's eyes glanced at the slave girl then back at the mirror as he tucked this needed information away. Very carefully he shaved and washed his face, his mind whirling with the opportunities that could await him if given half a chance, good food, and a better wardrobe.

Jake walked as stiffly as Corriger's tight grip on his arm allowed. When he had left the bathroom, she had immediately grabbed him and inspected him closely. He had been angry and embarrassed by her prodding and poking, especially when she had insisted he perform an enema on himself. It had taken just one more slap of Ann for him to obey, though he ground his teeth angrily as he did so.

The humiliation had not been merely from the fact that Ann was watching or that the general was forcing him, but from the fact that as the water filled him and then rushed out he found himself hard and aching for any type of touch. He hadretaliated by jerking off right onto the general's boots. His thoughts, however, had not been of revenge but of being abused by the cruel princess whose brand still marked his ass.

So now he was being shoved down the hallway, his arm twisted behind his back and up to the opposite shoulder, completely naked, his cheeks still red and burning from the slaps he had earned. A grin curled his lips as he made the march as difficult as he dared.

The general opened the door with one hand and shoved him through so that he landed on his side. The carpeted floor was a light green, the color called Sea Foam in the catalogs his mother used to collect and read before turning them in for a recycling fee. "Stand up, you fucking bastard!" Corriger yelled.

Jake looked around the room slowly without answering. The room was well lit, but no one else seemed to be waiting for them. He cried out between clenched teeth as he was kicked in the ass. "Don't you remember, general? Beating me doesn't work much, at least not for you. Sure you don't want to go get a horse to tie me behind?" he tossed out with a sneer as he refused to look up at her.

"Stand up, or I'll make Ann pay for your disrespect," Corriger threatened.

"Leave her out of it!" Jake yelled back.

The general readied to kick him again when a voice stopped her and caused the slave to sit up.

"Now, now, general. Is violence the only method you know?" The deep yet feminine voice was coming from behind a desk, large and modern looking, a computer sitting on it along with several monitors. The leather-covered chair with a high back was hiding the speaker. "There are so many other ways to get someone do as you wish," the voice continued.

Jake stood up as the chair rotated slowly. He placed his hands in front of his groin, suddenly too aware of his nakedness. This was not how he had planned to make a good impression on his new owner, and first impressions would dictate how easily controlled she could be. The voice didn't sound old, so he just hoped the face would be average and not ugly, though it would hardly matter if he got what he wanted.

"Money, power, love, blackmail," the voice rattled on. "These are all other methods that can be used to elicit the choice you wish the person to make."

The chair stopped, and Jake opened his mouth slightly as he saw the woman. Her features were familiar, and for a moment he was ready to throw himself on the floor and crawl the distance to the boots he loved so well. But the hair was much longer, braided into two plaits and even darker red. The eyes, too, were larger, and the face fuller. The clothing wasn't military at all; it looked like an elegant suit, the coat green and the shirt underneath black to set off the pale skin; both reflected the light as silk might. This was a person who didn't spend her time outdoors on raids or murder runs.

In her hands, the nails far better manicured than the Butcher's had ever been, was a rat. Not one of the white ones folks kept as pets, but one of the mangy ones that plagued the cities and the poor. Its muzzle was taped shut, and the woman patted its trembling head as she spoke, one hand wrapped gently around the body. "But I suppose that Yvonne never used much that wasn't physical. She just can't live in the real world, where we're all forced to deal with one another's decisions, their choices affecting our own."

Jake shuddered as the woman's hands moved quickly and he heard a tiny snap from the rat's now-motionless body.

"I agree that violence is sometimes necessary," the woman said. She looked at the dead rat with a sad frown before tossing it to the general, who caught it with a disgusted groan. "Isn't that correct, Jake?" the woman said as she leaned forward, placing her arms onto her desk.

At this distance, it was like looking into the past as a younger Butcher smiled at him. Jake only swallowed, afraid to do anything else for several minutes while the younger Yvonne stared at him. Her eyes were green like the queen's, her nose was regal like the king's, and her voice was deep and steady like Yvonne's.

The woman leaned back with a laugh. She stood up and

approached Jake. Now he saw that she was taller than Yvonne had been and wider; she wore black pants and soft-looking black shoes; her hair was in three braids, not the normal two he'd assumed. She looked him directly in the eyes as she dropped the bomb. "I'm Angelique. Yvonne's little sister. Now," she continued speaking as she backed up and motioned to a chair by the desk, "please do sit down."

Jake looked behind him and found himself alone in the room. Months ago he would have tried the door or the window, but something in the eyes told him that Angelique's security would be as thorough as Yvonne's. He sat down then, crossing his legs to hide himself from her view. It seemed like incest somehow to be seen by his Mistress' kid sister.

He waited silently as the second princess regarded him and closed down her computers. The younger princess leaned back in her chair, hands behind her head, and just looked at him. After watching her stare for several minutes, Jake finally spoke. "So, I've been given to you, your majesty?"

Angelique laughed again. "Oh, no. I've had you stolen or rescued depending on your point of view," she said.

Jake just frowned and watched as she laughed. Part of him wanted to thank her, while the other part wanted to call his real owner's room. After a moment he leaned forward. "Are we still in the palace?"

"Yes, but she can't find you," Angelique said. There was calmness in her face, but a mad joy radiated from her voice. "She's had three people killed since you disappeared five days ago."

"She's looking for me?" he asked, a desperate hope in every fiber of his being.

"Yes," Angelique stated more seriously. "Not because she cares about you. You do realize that, don't you? She was enjoying watching you die, slowly, agonizingly. You do know that?"

Jake slumped back into his chair and nodded. So here he was, kidnapped but perhaps rescued, if she was telling the truth. No sibling had been mentioned by Yvonne, the king or the queen in his hearing. Vaguely he remembered some news clips that had mentioned a younger princess, something about college or an ambassadorship too, but those images were old in his mind. He sighed and decided to play along.

"Yes, I know that, Your Majesty."

"Good. Then you will accept me as your new owner?" Angelique asked. Her green eyes narrowed.

"I haven't much choice, My Lady," Jake said as he stood up. He placed his hands behind his back as he stood straight.

Angelique also stood. "There are always choices," she stated flatly.

True to her word, Angelique was now standing off to one side watching silently as Jake looked at the three sets of clothes that were lying on her bed. The clothing was very much like that which he'd worn in the camp: soft, rich, the comforts of a slavery steeped in more than mere menial tasks. Jake ran his hands through his hair. Oddly, it had not been cut, so the spiky design he'd grown used to was now slightly wavy. "I get to choose?" he asked with a glance at her.

Angelique nodded. "If you don't like any of them..."

"Oh, no, that's not it," Jake countered quickly. "I'm just wondering which you'd prefer," he stated with a smile meant to charm.

"I like all of them; that's why they're here in the first place," Angelique said as she removed her jacket and tossed it onto the divan sitting by the window.

The tank top she wore showed that underneath, what had at first appeared softer and rounder than the heir's was instead stronger, thicker; her entire body now seemed leaner as well, and it struck Jake as slightly funny. Little Sister wasn't little in any sense of the word. He picked up the middle shirt and focused on it to keep from laughing. He held it up. "Think this tan color will show off my eyes?" he asked with a grin.

"It's taupe," Angelique corrected. "Looks fine. If you wish you may keep the others as well; just hang them up in there," she added as she walked past him and tapped on the door of a wardrobe. "I'll be back in about half an hour," she added as she left the room.

Jake waited until he had heard another door open and close, then bolted to the windows. Both were locked, but no shock sent him flying as had happened in the heir's suite. The two suites were almost identical: office below, with a spiral staircase leading up to the bedroom. The rooms were quite different, though. Black, clearly, was the primary color for both, probably because the national flag was black with a white royal coat of arms on it. But while Yvonne's suite was militant and blood red, this one had greens and browns in the nature designs on most of the black lacquered furniture.

Jake crossed the wooden floor to the front door and found it locked as well but not electrified as he'd expected. Standing near the door he noticed the first weapons in the room. Two sticks; *no, staffs,* he corrected himself, as he walked toward them. They were set on pegs in one wall, and underneath were several daggers with richly decorated wooden handles. On a small table under them was a statue of a female being with eight arms who seemed to be regarding him seriously.

Jake shuddered and stepped back. *Just stick around and play this out,* he cautioned himself. He pulled on the clothing and it all fit him well, even the sandals. As he buttoned up the shirt his fingers brushed his leather and metal collar, and he sighed, remembering how used to it he had become. Somewhere in his mind his conscience was telling him to scream and rip it from his throat. His hands, however, didn't know how to do that anymore, and the rest of his mind informed him that there was little point.

His wardrobe had a black bag sitting in the bottom, he discovered when he went to place the other two sets of clothes inside. After hanging things up he pulled it out and set it on the floor. It looked very familiar, the scent of the leather making him quake with memories he had tried to give up when death had seemed around the corner. Inside he found the items which had become far too much a part of his life.

"Are those yours?" Angelique's voice made him look up. She was standing there, her hair combed down around her head and her face still damp, a towel wrapped around her. "Yvonne threw those out a few weeks back when she returned from her last campaign. I thought they might have something to do with you," she added as she flipped the sides of her hair back with a comb and snapped barrettes into place.

"She threw them out?" Jake heard himself ask, then bit his lip as he zipped the bag back up.

"Sure; that is her usual pattern of behavior after she gets rid of a slave," Angelique said.

Jake was silent as she walked out of sight again. *Idiot! You didn't actually think you were special, did you?* he cursed himself as he put the bag back into the wardrobe. He examined the wardrobe closely but found nothing else except a pair of brown silk pajamas and a shaving case in the one drawer at the bottom. Simple but elegant — there was a theme here, he suspected.

Jake was looking at the bed, noting that there were further similarities between Angelique and the heir in the form of cuffs attached to the posts at head and foot. Unlike Yvonne's rough metal and leather, though, these were padded leather he discovered as he ran his hands over one and tried it on his wrist.

"You interested in things like that?" It was Angelique's voice again. This time she was in a green dress that clung to her body, the neckline plunging low to show off ample cleavage. She chuckled as the slave set the cuff down, stood up, and swallowed at her. "Not quite my sister's style, huh?" she said, making a turn.

"No, not at all," Jake said, then looked down while hastening to add, "My Lady."

"You may call me Mistress if you prefer," Angelique offered as she opened a matching handbag and looked inside.

"Is that an order?" he asked, an edge he didn't really mean in his voice.

Angelique grinned. "No, just another choice for you."

"And if I decide to just call you My Lady, what will you do to me or have done to me?" he asked bluntly.

She moved far more quickly that he could have imagined her heels would allow and was standing directly in front of him. "Nothing," Angelique said as she touched his shoulders with her hands. He flinched at the contact, and she clicked her tongue. "My actions are based on yours; nothing will happen to you here that you don't ask for one way or another," she explained.

Jake blinked, then set his mouth as his old dislike of those with more than himself surfaced. "What's to keep me from walking out of here or hurting you?"

The grin broke into a chuckle as Angelique slid her hand down one of his arms. "Why, your promise to obey me as your owner," she said. Suddenly she moved, and Jake found himself slammed face down onto her bed, his arm twisted violently behind his back. "Unless you're confirming the stereotype that a drug dealer's word is nothing but a pack of lies?" she challenged lightly as she pushed up on his arm, causing him to cry out.

Jake took a deep breath as he tried to figure out what had just happened. As his arm was twisted more he answered, "No, I will obey you, My Lady." He lay there as she released his arm and the bed moved slightly beneath him. When she touched his cheek, he pulled back but just far enough to watch her as she sat down next to where he lay. She sat so calmly, one leg crossed over the other at the knee so the slit in her dress went up to her thigh, that serene look on her face betrayed only by the gleam in her eyes. "Unless your sister finds me and reclaims me, I am your slave now," he added.

The green eyes rolled up toward the ceiling as though considering the possibilities in his words. Then Angelique stood up and walked to the main door. She turned after opening it. "I'll bring you back something to eat. Please feel free to look around and make yourself at home, Jake."

What the fuck? Jake laid flat on the bed, breathing slowly and moving his arm slightly. It hurt, but at least it moved, so it wasn't broken. As he relaxed he noticed that the canopy overheard continued the nature theme. There above him was a stream set near grove of trees, with deer and other animals drinking while a group of women watched from their position deeper in the woods. Behind them there was a deer roasting on a spit over a fire while one woman, her hair reddish and in braids, looked blissfully at the flames. He sat up and looked more closely at that woman with red hair; her fingers were at her lips. "Ugh," he said as he realized she was tasting the blood on her hand.

"This is more scary than my mistress' room," he told the empty room as he stood up. *What would she do if I found her, let her know where I was, offered myself to her?* he asked himself as he looked out the locked window. A lump of ice-cold fear formed in the pit of his stomach, making him shiver. He looked at the staircase, then headed for it and the office below.

The royal dinner table was quiet until the last dish had been set on the table and the servants and slaves dismissed by the queen. The heir in dress military uniform leaned across the table. "What are you doing back here?" she asked, sounding both angry and surprised. "I thought you were off on some diplomatic mission bullshit."

"Yvonne, please!" the queen said, her genteel face blushing deeply.

As the heir was about to speak, the king slammed his fist down on the table, making all three pairs of female eyes swing toward him. "Enough! You two act as though you were still children, which you are not!"

"Forgive me, father," Yvonne said with an incline of her head. "I'm simply surprised by Angelique's presence. I'm normally informed of all guests at the palace," she added with a glare toward the king.

"You were informed of this as well, but you've been paying little attention to things outside your own private dungeon," the king replied, breaking off to cough several times, causing the queen to rise from her seat and hurry toward him. "I'm fine; stop hovering," he said with difficulty. The women were silent as the queen returned to her seat, the youngest daughter reaching over the table and taking her mother's hand.

"It sounds worse," Yvonne commented slowly.

"Yes," the king stated. He held up his hand so that no one interrupted him. "Now I need to have a meeting with the both of you. Angelique has done very well in the West and across the seas in that direction. You need to be informed of this, Yvonne. She is to be your chief advisor and will have a place on the counsel," he reminded them all.

Yvonne frowned and muttered something under her breath.

"It is my wish, so it shall be done!" the king ordered.

"Don't worry, sister," Angelique said with a warm smile. "You are the heir."

"Who you'd like to see removed for your own benefit," Yvonne snarled. The calm she held like a dagger over everyone's head had vanished in the past five days. The appearance of the one person she truly detested here certainly didn't help. "But you're not strong enough to rule, and you know it," the heir added with a sneer as she sat back in her chair.

"Stop it!" the king bellowed, which set off another fit of coughing. He picked up his napkin, and when he removed it from his mouth the queen gasped and stood up. The king shook his head as his youngest daughter's eyes widened at the sight of the blood. "You see now why I recalled you," he said as he swallowed and winced at the pain in his chest.

"Yes, father," Angelique said softly. "You will have no problems with me as long as Yvonne chooses to treat me with sisterly respect," she added with a direct look into the dark eyes opposite hers. "I merely wish to do my duty to parents, king, and state. To obey and enforce the law, that is my highest duty to you all."

Yvonne rolled her eyes and turned to her food. Out of the corner of her eye she watched her father's slowed movements. The ring which marked her as heir seemed to itch a bit as she considered the near future. Her mind, however, was cursing the fact that this meeting about trade and peace would keep her from her scheduled questioning in the dungeon. She narrowed her eyes at her sister as the kid smiled and laughed at the story their mother told her about her latest foolish shopping trip. The Butcher was surrounded by fools, dying old men, and thieves. Deal first with one, and then the others.

Jake tapped his finger against each book as he read the titles silently. A search of both the office and the bedroom suite confirmed that the layout was much the same as the other princess', right down to the electronic devices for pulleys and so forth around the bed itself. The servants' entrance was locked and the telephones disconnected. No fancy electrical shocks, no guards waiting outside on the balcony, just simple locks. He was still a slave; this one was just more subtle about it.

Most of the books looked academic, boring and beyond his understanding or interest. Some words he recognized like "history," "philosophy," and "science," but there were other words he didn't really understand, though he could read them. The books lined two of the four walls completely as far as the needed doors, stairway, and window allowed. It was like one of those old libraries they sometimes showed on television, the ones only the rich had or the fairly well-off could afford cards to.

Her desk was unlocked, and that surprised him greatly. He'd have been beaten within an inch of his life for even looking into the desks of any of the others who'd owned him; Yvonne would have just killed him outright. *That's what I should have done then*, he decided with a disappointed sigh. The desk contents weren't interesting at first glance. Normal desk things, his knowledge once more based on television shows he had seen, like pens, pencils, paper, disks for the computer, scissors. Then a few more intriguing items like an address book with places he knew to be incredibly far away and others he'd never even heard of. There was even a mini refrigerator to one side about the size of a six pack.

In the bottom drawer of the desk, right underneath the computer keyboard arm, were three large books. When he removed them his sight fell on images of several people, all handsome, all almost entirely nude, and all restrained by various means, the chief of which were webs made of rope. The books had no titles, only dates on their covers, and when he opened them he found more pictures, identified by names and dates. There was no other text, only the captured men and a rare woman or two, and unlike the picture books Yvonne kept these captives all smiled back at him from beneath the protective plastic.

"There you are!"

The voice made Jake bolt and hit his head on the desk so that he rolled out onto his side, clutching at the bump forming there. He released the book he'd been looking at into unfamiliar hands, then accepted their aid in getting him to his feet.

"Didn't mean to scare you quite so much," the voice said. It was masculine so Jake opened his eyes. "Do you feel dizzy?" the man asked.

Jake nodded a bit and let the man sit him down in the window seat. He watched silently as the man knelt and returned the books to their place. This unfamiliar man was about his own size, his hair blond and his skin well tanned. When he looked up at Jake there was an amused twinkle in his blue eyes.

"Let's get back upstairs," the man said as he rose to his feet. He wore simple clothes but had no collar around his neck marking him as a slave. The clothes were not the uniform of the servants in the palace either, so Jake was wary. "Come on, I'll explain a few things once we're back upstairs," the man promised.

Jake silently went up the stairs in front of the other man. He took a deep breath and was about to ask some questions when a hand was pressed against his mouth. A cloth was forced between his lips and teeth and tied tightly behind his head. He grunted as the man pushed him forward onto the bed. If there was one thing Jake feared more than death in the dungeon it was another rape by another man. He braced his legs and struggled as his hands were likewise tied behind him. When he was pushed onto his side he glared at the man and tried to kick at him.

"Calm down," the man said. "Look," he explained as he held up his hands and stepped back, "I don't want to hurt you. I just need you to be quiet for a while."

Jake grunted, then stopped as he heard the door to the office below open. He heard two sets of footsteps, one the click of high heels and the other the sound of boots.

"Please don't make any noise," the man begged him softly as he sat down on top of him, his hand placed over the gag.

The voices were quite clear, and Jake closed his eyes when the rough, firm voice of Yvonne confirmed his hopes and fears.

"So do you have anything to drink around here?"

He heard the sound of the refrigerator opening. "I have mineral water, cranberry juice, orange juice," Angelique replied.

"Orange juice? Really?" Yvonne asked. There was the sound of something thudding against flesh. "Where'd you get this?"

"Part of the perks of being an ambassador," Angelique replied. The refrigerator shut again. There was a silence. "So what do you want, Yvonne?"

"Damn this is good!" Another pause. "I want to ask you if you enjoy your foreign work?" Yvonne finally said.

There was a creak and squeak as though a chair was being moved. "Very much. Why; you want to make sure you take away the things I enjoy most when you become queen?" Angelique's voice was flat and direct.

"Quite the contrary, little sister. I would like you to become the minister of foreign affairs." Yvonne's voice had that drip of sweetness she'd used on rare occasions, and it made Jake twist a bit in his captor's grip.

"What's that?" Yvonne immediately asked. "Who's upstairs?"

"Shawn! Would you come down here, darling?" Angelique's voice was calm.

The man looked at Jake, then backed away. Jake just watched silently as the blond head disappeared below the floor. For a few seconds his mind flirted with the idea of crying out or crawling to the stairs, but he just stayed still, listening for the perfect time.

"What's this?" Yvonne asked. The sound of her boots meant that she must have been circling the man with her predatory stare.

"Who's this?" Angelique corrected. "This is Shawn, the companion I picked up in the California Republic."

"Companion? You mean slave," Yvonne stated. "Where's his collar, or don't they do that in California?"

"I did not misspeak," Angelique said. A silence followed.

"He can't be from a ruling family," Yvonne said.

"There are no ruling families with us," the man said.

Jake tensed as he heard the low growl in Yvonne's throat, a sign that she was displeased but controlling it. "Then you'd best remember that here we do have ruling families, and while here you will treat us with respect," she threatened.

"I meant no offense, your majesty," the man replied.

"Are you jealous, sister?" Angelique asked with a tinkle of laughter in her voice. "I take it from Father's comments that you have not found your slave?"

"Not yet, but it will be soon," Yvonne snapped.

"I'm surprised that it has taken so long. Over a week, isn't it?" Angelique added. "I am so disappointed in you, big sister."

"I need not impress you. It is you who must impress me," Yvonne replied. There was some silence and then the sound of glass clicking on wood. "Father is impressed with your diplomatic skills. I'm satisfied."

"What more do you want?" Angelique asked.

"Everything," Yvonne said with a chuckle. "Goodnight, little sister."

Jake sat up on the bed as the door closed below. He shook his head, sending the beads of sweat which had formed there flying. He looked up just as the man rose into the room via the staircase. After the gag was removed, he swallowed the spit that had built up in his mouth.

"Thank you for not making a scene," Angelique said as she passed the bed.

Jake turned his head to watch her disappear behind the hallway into the bathroom. His head swung back as he felt his hands untied. "Who are you?"

"I'm Shawn," the man said. He stood up straight and raised his hands in front of him. "Rub them like this; it will help the circulation," he instructed as he rubbed one wrist with the opposite palm, then switched. "Hope I didn't hurt you so much."

"He's had much worse I'm sure," Angelique replied as she returned. Now dressed in green pajamas, she embraced the blond man. Her green eyes remained focused on Jake as she allowed her companion to hug and caress her for several minutes. "So what was he doing when you found him?" she asked as she very gently pushed the blond back.

"Going through the desk, like you knew he would," Shawn said as he rubbed the back of his neck. Against his groin the fabric of his simple pants had grown taut; the look in his eyes darkened as the princess approached Jake.

Jake moved back so that he was sitting on the edge of the bed as the princess joined him. She crossed her legs at the knees and placed one hand on his knee. "My desk, huh? Find anything of interest there?"

"Yeah, the refrigerator, the books," Jake began. He glanced up as the blond stepped behind the princess.

"I can tie him up for the night to make sure he doesn't run out and get your sister," Shawn suggested, his hands in fists as her hand slipped farther up Jake's leg.

Jake looked into her green eyes which were dark and narrowed. His body tingled as her hand caressed his thigh. He screamed as she spun, and a line of red blocked his vision for a second. "What?" he cried out as he stepped back. His leg ached, and he saw a thin line of blood seeping through his pants.

"I, uh," the blond sputtered as he dropped to his knees. Jake stepped back, clenching at his stomach as the man toppled over and a stream of blood flowed from his head.

Angelique turned to the slave and showed him the knife she had had hidden in her hand, under her pajama top. "I really hate jealousy," she said with a sigh. "Folks who are jealous are rarely loyal. Disloyalty cannot be allowed; too dangerous at this point in the plan. Choosing to be disloyal would a poor choice, Jake."

Jake just stood there breathing heavily. He turned as she propelled him to the bed. He crawled underneath as directed and watched as she rang the servants' bell and spoke into the intercom. Soon several pairs of bare feet and one shod pair appeared from the direction of the slaves' entrance. The slaves pulled the body out then cleaned the floor quickly and silently.

Angelique's green eyes looked under the bed, her hair slapping down on the floor. "You may come out now. They're gone."

Jake raised himself from the floor after crawling out. The floor was perfectly clean; there was no sign of the murder that was just committed. "They'll tell my mistress," he whispered, then tensed for a slap which never came. When he glanced up the green eyes were twinkling back at him over a grin.

"That would be a choice — the incorrect choice," Angelique said. Her eyes slid down to his leg, causing her to frown. "You'd best take care of the leg," she instructed with a nod toward the bathroom. As he went in the direction indicated she called after him, "Don't be like Shawn."

Jake paused, then bowed his body slowly, then rose again. "Yes, My Lady."

The cut wasn't deep, and the bleeding had already stopped. The material of the pants would need to be soaked, he realized, so he took them off. The antiseptic stung as he applied it and a bandage to the wound. No, the cut wasn't what hurt, really; it was the surprise at what he'd witnessed that made him shake even now.

He jumped, knocking his knee into the sink, when Angelique's face appeared in the mirror.

"I thought you could use these," she simply stated, that smile on her face indicating that she was amused, as she tossed the brown pajamas to him.

She was gone before he could speak. Jake looked into the mirror at his emaciated frame after removing his shirt. *I look worse than when I first got here*, he thought as he recalled the month-plus of starvation in Yvonne's hyper-guarded suite.

The strong image of the heir to the throne came to his mind: always ready for combat, a weapon within easy reach, her hands quick to administer punishment. Her voice was firm, the statements plain and simple, the joy evident when she humiliated him, the tremble of flames underneath her words as she angered. Her body was firm and lean — barely anything extra on her — displayed to make a man or woman weak from desire and fear. She was every dark damned fantasy he'd ever had; she was a slow, passionate death.

A giggle broke the images and replaced it with the full-figured little sister, her hair tumbling around her shoulders, her eyes lighted by the hidden thoughts behind the laughter. Nothing like he'd dreamed of, except when he'd been talking with his gang back in the city, an image of femininity none of them could see in mothers or girlfriends. A calmness echoing from each word, each step, each movement, shone from her. Around her there was a shadow of the two deaths he'd been allowed seen her bring with her bare hands.

Jake splashed his face with cold water to clear his head. He checked out his section of the storage cabinet, noting that everything he expected was there. So far she hadn't touched him, and her earlier words returned to his mind. He took out the razor and touched up his face, then splashed a bit of cologne on before dressing.

She was in bed reading when he entered the bedroom. The covers were tossed back so she could lean over a large book laid out before her. As he approached he could see it was one of the picture books he'd found below the desk. "Is this what you were looking at when Shawn found you?"

"Yes, My Lady. You said I could look around. I didn't pick any locks," Jake added.

Angelique's head turned up. "I didn't read about any thieving skills in your record," she simply stated before turning the page. Her gaze returned to the book. "You recognize him," she said, tapping the page with one manicured fingernail.

Jake went to the side of the bed nearest her and bent over to see. "Shawn?" he asked, a bit surprised.

She nodded, an almost sad look on her face, and turned the page several times, each page had the blond's picture on it. She stopped at the first blank page. "My collection," she sighed as she sat back and looked at the slave. She sniffed. "Cologne. Very nice."

Jake felt his body heat up at the compliment, his heartbeat thumping a bit louder in his ears. "You said I would get what I asked for, My Lady," he reminded her.

"Yes," Angelique agreed. She reached out and stroked his nearest hand. A chuckle rose in her throat as his cock poked up, expanding the pajamas. "Didn't my sister utilize her property?"

"Of course," Jake heard himself say, then cursed himself as he continued, "I miss that so much."

"You sound like you might be in love with her," Angelique sniffed.

Jake's body shook as the suggestion sent a wave of chill through him. "No, of course not," he answered. "She trained me very well though," he added in a whisper.

There was silence for a few moments, then she paged back the picture book to a particularly enticing image. "Did you ever do this with her?"

"No, My Lady," he said. Instead of a teasing reply or a sharp order to go fetch materials, she simply closed the book. He looked up as the covers were moved and she slid between them.

"That's too bad," Angelique told him. She pointed to the end of the bed. "There's a bedroll for you. Time to go to sleep, Jake."

"Yes, My Lady," he said as he moved away. At the end of the bed was a thin mattress rolled up around a pillow and a blanket. It was soft even on the hard wooden floors. From there he could see the edge of the canopy in the starlight filtering through the windows.

No chains, no guards, no bars on the windows, her just a few feet away. Jake remembered the tiny slave cells he'd been shoved into and the room he'd shared with three half-siblings in a tenement house in the city. The feeling of recalled shackles on him as he hung over the red and black silk covers made tears come to his eyes. *This is too much freedom.* His thoughts surprised him enough to make him sit up straight.

The promises the Butcher made and his days in the dungeon flooded his mind. Suddenly everywhere he looked he saw nothing but bars and traps. Beneath them was the pulse his blood vibrated with as he remembered each torture, each touch, each orgasm he'd felt, really truly felt, for the first time with her. He sobbed silently as he lay back down.

It wasn't that there was a plot to take over the kingdom, Jake discovered, so much as a plan that could be put into action if need be. Each day there was a meeting between Angelique, Corriger, and several household servants and staff. Among these he was surprised to see the woman doctor, the girl Betty from the kitchen, and even the chief stablehand. He learned from the doctor that Yvonne had gone back on several promises made to each of them.

Phone calls came in as well which made Angelique nod and take down notes that only Corriger was allowed to see. Jake stood in the office off to one side during all of this, his presence ignored most of the time. Every now and then Angelique would direct a question toward him. Usually these were about Yvonne's daily habits, the number of weapons that might be hidden out of sight in her room, things which they thought someone who had been so close to her might know that General Corriger apparently did not.

Jake would answer as completely as he could, though he felt he was the biggest Judas in the world while he did so. The words of a man who'd claimed to be his father would ring in his ears: "If you're going to hell already, what does one more sin matter?" Other words Yvonne herself drilled into him made each piece of information he gave feel like a knife: "You don't exist except for me, slave."

With each day that passed his image in the bathroom mirror grew firmer and healthier, making her words less real. Then he'd remember the number of troops and loyal guards Yvonne controlled. According to the staff and slaves that number seemed to be lessening but which was still huge. On one such day, as he stood in the bathroom after a particularly tiring meeting, he sighed and stepped back from the mirror and into the shower to clean up.

About an hour later he presented himself nude to Angelique, a coil of rope he'd found in her clothes closet in his hands. "My Lady," he began, he still could not say the words he sensed she truly wanted. The old brand with Yvonne's particular twist on the royal crest had been removed a few days after he was introduced to the younger princess, but Yvonne's implanted status still burned in every cell of his body.

Angelique looked up from the statue she was holding. She smiled, then held it toward him. "There are many paths for each of us," she said as she touched the hands of the figure. "Each one based on our desires, on our means, on our ability. But they should also be based on knowledge, because, once chosen, the path determines which choices are available next."

She set the statue down, then crossed to sit on the end of her bed. "Why did you become a drug dealer, Jake?"

The slave blinked and stepped back. Here he was, offering himself to her in a way he had thought would please her, and she asked him such a non-erotic question. It didn't take more than a minute for him to come up with an answer. "I've always desired to be a slave. That was a way to get my desires."

Angelique tilted her head, then shook it. "Really? Are you sure you're not just repeating what my dear sister wished to hear?"

"The law is the law," he began, sudden doubts rising in his mind. "I knew the law; I knew the consequences. I made a choice, My Lady, and I got what I deserved."

"True," Angelique agreed. "That doesn't answer my question, however." Instead of pressing for further conversation she stood up and took the rope from him. "Now you will get some knowledge about yourself."

Jake looked down at the web of white robe that bound him between the two rings hanging from the ceiling. He could barely feel it touching him, and none of it was tight, yet he couldn't move a muscle beyond his head, fingers, and toes.

Angelique had shed her clothing and was standing looking at him. Her skin glistened with perspiration from her hours of work. She lifted her braids and fastened them on top of her head with two large pins.

Jake's cock grew as much as it could, wrapped as it was in the coil of rope and pulled back toward his own ass. He watched her breasts lift as she worked with her hair, then bounce slightly, the pectoral muscles giving them a firm shape as she lowered her arms. Swallowing, he allowed himself to speak his thoughts. "You are so beautiful, My Lady."

Her lips smiled and parted as her tongue darted out to lick them. This seduction was completely unlike anything he had experienced. She need not have played to his visual senses, for her word and the fear that he could be killed at any moment would have been enough to have him between her legs after what her sister had put him through. As her tongue made a round circuit of her full lips her eyes swept over his body. "Very nice work," she told herself as she moved closer.

Jake sighed as he felt the heat from her body rush around him. Her hands sent jolts through his flesh even when they touched merely the rope. At some point he had become the rope, the rope being his only means of standing on his feet as his body went limp with desire, the rope, and therefore himself, her instrument, subtle and strong like her. He gasped as she jerked his head back with his hair. The expected blade never met his throat, but her wet, coarse tongue traveled over the skin of one ear and then of the other. His gasps grew as her teeth pulled at one lobe.

"I think you like that," she whispered as she withdrew. She chuckled as Jake jerked his body in an attempt to regain contact with her. "Ah, but you offered yourself. Now you must accept the consequences," she reminded him. "Or must you?" she teased as she pinched a free inch of flesh on his buttocks.

"Yes," Jake gasped. He moaned as his cheeks, already parted by the rope, were shoved further apart by a wet digit. Weeks of disuse after months of constant torment made his body ache at the thought of what might happen next.

"Do you give yourself to me, Jake, or do I take it from you?" she whispered, adding a second finger inside of him.

In Jake's mind his body seemed to shrink down to the area around his asshole. The ropes seemed non-existent, her fingers his only support. He heard the question repeated, so he replied in words mixed with gasps as the feelings pulled him within himself. "Take it, Jake is yours, My Lady," he cried out.

A sigh was his only reply as the fingers were pulled out and the ropes once more formed his world. Jake turned his head and saw Angelique wipe her hands before pulling on a robe. He watched, his mouth opened, the words to plead for anything on his lips, as she moved to stand in front of him.

The words he said made little difference as she untied and expertly recoiled the ropes. While the setup had taken a few hours, the removal was far quicker, and soon Jake was swaying a bit at the pressure his body placed on his legs. Angelique's eyes were pale as she shook her head at him, tossed the rope onto her bed, and walked away.

"My Lady. What did your slave do?" he began as he took two steps forward, then started to fall. He balanced himself on one knee and his hands, watching her retreat down the hallway. "Mistress," he whispered; the word still caught in his chest. He shook his head as he lowered himself to the ground.

Jake rubbed his body, which was covered with gooseflesh from the lack of blood to all his body but his cock and balls. Turning toward the balcony he blinked and held his breath. The air was chilly because the doors were opened, the curtains billowing in the night breeze.

He stood up and went to the balcony and out into the darkness. The moon above was a crescent of faded yellow against the points of white twinkling around it. Never had he been allowed out on the Butcher's balcony, not even after he had been certain he had proved his loyalty. His cock, which should have been withering in the cool breeze, brushed against his abdomen as it grew.

He could leave, take that rope lying on the bed and climb down, run out into the night and away from the insanity that would break out as soon as the king died. The world was so much larger than he had realized. Then a figure on a horse belowcaught his eye, and he backed against the wall. The Butcher dismounted, slapped the stable boy twice, then stormed into the palace and out of sight. His cock should have been bursting now, but instead it had retreated in fear.

"I wonder if you can understand?" Angelique's voice behind him made Jake turn. She was dressed in her pajamas, her hair loose around her shoulders.

Jake looked down at his bare feet, then back up at the princess. "I don't think I do," he said, pleading silently for the answers that would take him from hiding and bind him to her.

"I won't tell you what to think. I'm not her," Angelique said.

Corriger, however, was neither as kind nor as concerned with Jake's humanity. She was having enormous fun dictating how and when Jake and Ann would amuse themselves and the free women. On all of the previous nights Jake would have begged for any type of sexual contact, but Angelique hadn't responded to his offers as long as he could not call her Mistress. Now in the middle of the fourth forced fuck with Ann he was wishing it would end, as was the slave girl.

Corriger and her slave had come to Angelique's office late with several sealed envelopes. The contents had greatly upset the princess, and she gone on a rampage for almost an hour. The documents were copies of drafts for new laws Yvonne would issue after the king's death, a loss that seemed certain to occur before the week ended. Each law, in the youngest princess' words, "immorally infringed on the rights of citizens." The proposed changes included expanding the enslavement penalty to the offspring of those convicted if born after sentence was passed, confiscation of property as a penalty for discussion and trade with enemies of the state, which meant any nation not having a treaty with the United Eastern States, and state control over all video media.

After literally breaking the window in her office with her fist, Angelique had been forced to retire to her bedroom by Corriger. To calm the princess, Corriger directed the two slaves too put on a good show, primarily consisting of Jake's performing various sexual acts on Ann. The slave girl seemed to enjoy the attention at first, but as he offered his cock to her mouth for the third time Jake could see tears forming in her eyes.

"I can't do this," Jake announced as he pulled away and stood up.

"You will until I decide otherwise!" Corriger ordered in a yell that made Ann cringe in terror.

"It's hurting her!" Jake replied as he picked his clothes up from the floor. "If you want to hurt her, you do it; I won't."

Corriger rose to her feet, swaying a bit from the alcohol she'd been consuming during the show. "You're forcing me to hurt her, slave! Do you enjoy seeing her beaten in front of you?"

"Jake, please," Ann whispered as she was pulled up by her hair.

His heart pounding, Jake knelt before the princess. "My Lady, please," he begged.

Angelique's faded eyes looked at him from under the hand she'd had over her eyes for the last several minutes. "General, take your girl and leave. I have a headache," the princess added before Corriger could object.

"As you wish, Your Majesty," Corriger replied as she released her slave by shoving her toward her own pile of clothing on the floor. "I'm sorry you were not amused by these two."

Angelique just nodded and stood up with a wave toward the door.

Jake watched as the general steered Ann out the door, the slave girl clenching her clothing to her body. Once the door was closed behind them he looked up at the princess. "Thank you, My Lady."

"I do have a headache," Angelique said.

"Is there anything your slave can do to ease it?" Jake asked as he sat up on his knees.

The princess merely sighed, shaking her head, then walked toward the bathroom. Jake stayed on his knees for a few moments, trying to force that one word out of his mouth. He gave up when he caught the multi-armed goddess regarding him with what now seemed like a sad smile. Some days he would have sworn that statue was alive since the little face seemed to hold every imaginable expression.

Jake's cock ached as he pulled his pants off, not from arousal but from over-use. *That's something I never thought could happen,* he thought as he put his pajamas on. He considered the canopied bed after donning the pajama top. The sound of the shower ended as he made a decision. The bed sheets were soft, but not satin as Yvonne's had been. He folded down a corner on the side she'd been sleeping on and stacked the quilt at the foot of the bed. He'd just finished laying out his own bedding when Angelique tapped him on the shoulder.

"Thank you," she simply said with a tired smile.

The slave nodded. After the princess was in bed, the covers tucked around her so that one arm rested outside and the other cradled her head, Jake knelt at the edge. "Is there nothing your slave can do for you, My Lady?"

"You know what that is," Angelique said. She waved him away when he could only open and close his mouth a few times without success. "She still owns you. How very sad for you."

Jake blinked. He waited a few moments as he gazed upon her face, her closed eyes and a tiny sleepy expression making her seem far more fragile that he knew she was. He crawled to the end of the bed and lay down himself. As his hand brushed his cock when he scratched his thigh, he noted with amazement that it was hard again. Odd, because he didn't really feel aroused in any usual way. He decided it was just his body betraying him, something he should have been used to after months with the Butcher. That thought, however, made him limp and eager for sleep.

The next three days were devoted to more meetings, with Jake's role further reduced to fetching drinks for people and answering the slaves' entrance when food was brought. At first, he'd flattered himself into thinking that the atrocities that Yvonne was accused of were a result of losing him. But the list reached back farther, to before he had even been enslaved. Her pleasure in torturing him was not unique. Her excursions into the cities had been for pleasure, and the reported drafts of her new laws proved that she intended to continue to rule with an iron fist.

Nothing was ever said about what the Butcher had done to her sister to earn the dangerous hatred that blazed behind those green eyes whenever Jake found Angelique looking at pictures of the royal family. It was true that Jake himself had been the final cause of Corriger's dismissal, but the general had complaints galore and very few compliments. Betty and the chief stablehand had come into the conspiracy last, after Yvonne had sent away Mike, the promised husband for the kitchen maid, for no reason, other than to see the poor girl weep.

Jake was standing off in one corner just listening when a call came. Angelique told everyone to stay where they were, and soon they were joined by the chief steward. The man barely gave Jake a second glance, nor did he seem surprised to find Corriger standing next to the princess. Jake couldn't believe the words coming from the steward's mouth.

"The Queen Mother has sent me to you, Princess Angelique, to inform you of His Majesty the King's death." The entire room was quiet as Angelique moved around her desk, motioning for the steward to continue. "The Queen Mother wishes to know when you will be moving against your sister."

"What are you talking about, old man?" Corriger began until Angelique held up her hand.

"Is there proof?" the princess simply asked.

The chief steward nodded and returned to the door. The doctor who had primarily cared for Jake entered now, carrying a folder in her hand. "I have the test results," the doctor said.

Angelique took the offered documents and read them, then handed them to Corriger. "How do you know she arranged this?"

The doctor grew very pale, but she spoke with only a slight quiver in her voice. "I gave her the poison myself. I told her how to administer it. Just as you instructed."

Jake took the folder from the chief stablehand and looked at the enclosed blood tests. The king had died of hemorrhaging. There were medical terms he couldn't understand, but the conversation indicated that Yvonne was to blame.

Angelique put her arm around the doctor's shoulder. "You'll be taken care of, my dear doctor. Don't worry. Just be patient."

"She must know," the doctor responded. "She knows everything that goes on around here. She'll kill us all."

"So she'll kill us a little sooner than she would have anyway," Corriger stated. She turned to Jake with narrowed eyes and a cocked grin. "Or a little later for others."

No one said anything as Jake bolted up the staircase. The balcony doors were open, and he sought refuge there. The dark night was pierced over and over by crying and screaming, and by bells tolling the death of the king. On every television set the announcement would be made. At first there would be riots and parties in the street, the poor people celebrating a slight victory by simply surviving their oppressors. The announcements of Yvonne's succession would end all such celebrations very soon.

Jake ignored the chilly breeze as he leaned over the rail. Corriger had, of course, been correct. He would die soon. The collar felt as though it was choking him, so he pushed one finger between it and his throat. He had begged her for death once, he had accepted it hanging in the dungeon, and now he looked down from the fourth floor, wondering if the fall would be a quick ending. His fingers pulled on his collar and he swore into the darkness. He couldn't even jump, because his body belonged to someone else. Instead he cursed himself and went to the bathroom.

Angelique had given him permission to use the bathroom whenever he wished, so he used that privilege now in an attempt to wash away the fear. Each time he closed his eyes, the image of cruel eyes and shoulder-length scarlet hair filled his mind, and behind them the words he'd burned into his mind. *Jake doesn't exist except for you.* Jake washed himself slowly, no longer trying to block the memories he had been blocking ever since his failed attempt to seduce the younger princess.

The water fell over his body; the soap slipped upon his flesh. The razor tingled his skin as he carefully shaved each spot he could reach. Each day without fail he had used everything in the personal hygiene bag, and tonight he used them again. The enema reminded him of the humiliating thrill he had felt as Yvonne had watched him from her tub. He could almost picture her through the curtains, except these were not clear but mint green, and the bathtub was behind a screen.

His wrists ached as he reached up and placed his hands around the spout where they had been chained on many occasions. Holding himself in place, he could imagine how trapped he had felt, how aroused and how alive the vibrating dildo in his ass had made him feel on such occasions. Jake thrust forward and felt the heavy bounce of his cock. He sighed and rolled his head against one arm.

A chill swept over him, and his mind was dark. His hands were no longer holding the shower spout but were chained; the water was no longer hitting him, just drops that sounded in the darkness, Yvonne's voice in his head repeated a different sentence: *I'll just kill you when I tire of you.* He jumped back and found his hands at his sides, the tiles of the bathtub still around him, and the mint green curtain to one side. His cock hung firm and heavy until he pounded his head against the tiles.

"I hope you haven't broken anything." Angelique's voice made Jake turn around. Her head was poking through the far end of the curtain, looking at him with a sad frown. "Remembering good times or bad?" she asked.

"Both," Jake replied. He lowered his eyes, then raised them again. "Do you wish anything, My Lady?" he asked.

Angelique tilted her head before replying. "You wish to go back to her, don't you?"

Jake closed his eyes. *I'm a fool, a complete fool,* he told himself as he remained silent. He opened his eyes as the shower floor moved a bit to find her climbing naked into the shower. The tiles felt cool as he backed up as far as he could.

"You were fantasizing about her taking you back, correct?" Angelique asked as she stepped onto the tiny mint green fish that were pressed into the bottom of the shower to stop slips. "What were you thinking? What was she doing to you?"

"It was, kind of, a memory," Jake said slowly.

"I want to know," Angelique said as she moved under the stream of water, so close to him that he could smell the perfume she wore being washed away. Her hand grabbed his wrist and held it fast. "It had something to do with your wrists."

"Yes, My Lady. She handcuffed me to the showerhead and did whatever she wished to this body," he said as he looked at her fingernails. Her grip was firm but relaxed, her presence was calm and sure, and his breathing increased rapidly.

"And in your fantasy just now she did the same thing because she was so happy to have you back?"

"Yes, but . . ." Jake tried to pull his hand free, but found her grasp to be as strong as always. "I'd end up back in the dungeon on my way to death again."

"You still want to go back to her?" Angelique asked as she released his hand.

"She is my mistress still," he said, then jerked back as though she would strike him. The green eyes just regarded him seriously and quietly. "I wish it wasn't so, My Lady," Jake added as he bowed his head. He sighed as fingers crept through his wet hair, combing it out and patting his head.

"What do you wish was so?" Angelique whispered into the ear her caressing had uncovered.

Images ran through Jake's mind. A bigger apartment than the tenement he had been raised in was something he had had for a while. Rolls of hundreds in his pocket had become a reality. The look of fear in people's eyes when he told them the price had just increased. The desperate moaning of a woman screwing for a gram or two of whatever he was dealing at the moment. The feeling of the whip as it caught him on his ribs and the pressure as his ass was fucked. Each one of these had something he wanted or thought he wanted or had been told he wanted.

He raised his eyes and looked into hers. *Everyone has choices. I won't tell you what to think.* His knees felt weak; his body was both icy and burning at the same time. "May I please be excused, My Lady?" he begged with a whimper in his voice.

Angelique stepped back and pointed to the curtain. "You're not worth it," she said softly.

Jake blinked, then hurried from the shower and bathroom. Out on the balcony he cursed himself once more. He looked at the statue underneath the staffs near the balcony where Angelique prayed each morning. Each hand represented a choice and a path, each path branching off into other choices, both our own and others she had explained to him when he had asked.

After a few minutes he went to the door and tried the knob. It turned in his hands, and the door opened back into the bedroom suite. He was completely nude; the water had dried on his body, but his hair was still damp. Angelique didn't appear to tell him to stop or to tackle him, Corriger wasn't waiting outside for him. Jake stepped out onto the hallway carpet and closed the door behind him. The lock clicked, and he realized there was only one place for him to go now.

Yvonne barely looked up when he walked into her office on the other side of the palace. She glanced at him once, then sat back in her chair and returned her attention to the document she'd signed only minutes before.

Jake swallowed, then lowered himself to the floor, his arms and legs flat. Her boots appeared in front of his face a few minutes later. At her order he raised himself enough to lick them thoroughly. The texture beneath his lips, the taste of leather and dust, made him hard as he put all his attentions into them. He yelped when she grasped his hair and lifted him up to his knees.

"So, did my little sister treat you all right, slave?" Yvonne asked. She smiled when his face clouded with fear and surprise. "Oh, yes, I've known where you've been this entire time. Haven't I, Ann?"

Jake's eyes narrowed as the slave girl walked down the spiral staircase from the bedroom above. She was naked, her body marked with red welts and scratches, and Jake felt his cock shrink as any pity he had felt was replaced by anger. Ann moved to Yvonne's side and laid her head on the new queen's arm. "Yes, Mistress. Your slave hopes you are happy."

"No!" Jake screamed as he tried to stand up. His efforts ended with his lip bleeding from the blow the Butcher's hand dealt him. The forced had thrown him against a wall. "Your slave has returned to you, Mistress," he said as he rose to his knees.

"Yes, but you're not interesting any more," Yvonne said. She grabbed the slave girl by her smooth pubes, smiling as she cried out and opened her legs wider. "Now Ann, here, is much more interesting than you could ever be, drug dealer. No duty to punish only to enjoy."

Jake fought the tears that were building up in his eyes, threatening to blind him. He reached for the doorknob and was forced back by the shock he received.

"It's too late, slave," Yvonne said. She slapped Ann's ass, and the slave girl ran up the staircase. "But don't worry. I'll give you my full attention right after I've taken care of a few last-minute things."

Jake sobbed as he rubbed his burned hands. He looked up as Yvonne stood over him. "Ah, did you think you'd be forgiven? Sorry, you committed the crime; I'm merely carrying out justice," she said with a chuckle. "Something so many of my people have forgotten about lately. But that will change very soon."

Yvonne smiled as she noted that his cock was hard and edging up his stomach at the mere sight of her and the sound of her voice. She stepped very close and placed one boot between his legs, lifting his balls up with the tip of her foot.

Jake's breath caught in his throat as the feeling of leather and the power radiating from her overcame him. He pressed his lips together firmly to keep from begging, but a moan was building as she teased him by lowering and raising her foot.

"You'd come right now if I ordered you," Yvonne declared. She pulled her foot back and chuckled. "But I'm not going to."

Jake looked up and watched as she went up the staircase. Wrapping his arms around his bent legs he cursed himself as he rocked back and forth. He'd only had a few hours of sleep when the Butcher kicked him awake in the morning.

Jake stood still as the executions continued. First there had been the slaves and staff that had taken part in the conspiracy. None of them had begged for their lives, and most had cursed the new queen as she motioned and each head was severed. The Queen Mother sat on her throne in chains, Yvonne announcing that her mother would be allowed to live out her life in her room under guard after she saw what her foolishness had wrought and the number of deaths it was causing.

Most of the aristocracy had not been caught yet, but Jake had been forced to watch as the television announcements of rewards for their capture went out over the airways. Corriger walked up to the bloody block and spat toward Ann. Jake swallowed as the ax descended. His own death wouldn't be so easy, he was sure.

"Now for the final one of the day," Yvonne announced as she stood up.

Jake put his hands on his stomach as the younger princess was led out in chains. Though dressed in pajamas and slippers, just as she would have been after her shower, Angelique looked calm and certain of herself. Her eyes gazed directly at him and winked, causing Jake to blink in confusion.

"Do you so fear me, big sister, that you must entrust my death to your guards?" Angelique asked calmly.

Yvonne stepped down to the floor. "Fear you? You stupid little bitch. I've known what you've been doing for years. I allowed you to do it."

"Ah, I see," Angelique said with a sad grin. "Then I think it only right you control everything at the end, don't you?"

"No, you cannot. She is your sister!" the Queen Mother shouted. Jake rushed to protect the older woman who had had a few kind words for him but was thrown back by the guard, who slapped her down.

Yvonne turned toward the throne with a glare. "No one touches him but me!" Her eyes widened as the chains that linked her sister's wrists together suddenly encircled her throat.

Jake grabbed the traitor slave girl Ann and held her as she tried to join in the fight. "You little bitch; you lied to everyone, didn't you?" he growled as he forced her hands behind her back.

Angelique was strong, and her attack was unexpected, but it took Yvonne only a minute to toss her over her shoulder to land with a crunch across the bottom step leading to the thrones. The three red braids splayed out around her head, but there was no sound or movement. "I'll take you out, then, if that is your wish, little sister," Yvonne said as she took the ax from the executioner.

Jake pushed the slave girl to the floor and jumped down two steps. "Mistress, please!" he yelled, not knowing what to offer or to say but only thinking to delay things.

Yvonne glared up from where she stood over her sister. "Shut up!" Yvonne's eyes widened suddenly as she jerked her head upward. From her throat a dagger was sprouting, the red blood gushing out onto the carpet. She opened her mouth, but nothing issued forth but more blood.

"Release me!" the Queen Mother ordered, and after a moment the guards obeyed with mumbled apologies.

Angelique sat up, one hand to her head, and considered the body of her sister lying beside her. "Keys?" she asked suddenly.

Jake took the keys from the chief guard and hurried down. As he unlocked the shackles he kept looking at the Butcher, lying as she had laid out so many people before.

"She's quite dead," Angelique assured him. "I don't miss my mark even when I'm forced to use weapons. Thank you for giving me the distraction, Jake."

The slave looked into the new Queen's green eyes, then lowered his own. "What will you do with your slave?" he asked.

The green eyes went very cold, and the words spoken were like spears through his soul. "I haven't decided if I want him." Then she smiled and used him as a brace to help her stand. "Right now, I just want something to drink."

As they passed the weeping slave girl the new Queen stopped and wrapped an arm around the slim shaking shoulders. With her other hand she caressed the long brown hair. "Oh, Ann, you've become a traitor. I, of course, understand that Corriger mistreated you, and like a fool you thought my sister would treat you better. But even a slave must be loyal. And you've proved yourself disloyal."

Jake swallowed as he watched Angelique take the slave girl's head firmly in her hands. With one twist the sounds of Ann's weeping were cut short, as was her life. The new Queen sighed as she released the body, a look of exhaustion on her face. Jake simply stepped over the dead body and followed her out of the throne room to check on the condition of the palace.

That night as they watched the remaining slaves and staff clean up the throne room, Jake sat at the Queen's feet. Angelique touched her sister's throne announcing it was to be burnt. He held her goblet for her without being ordered to, pouring her more when she returned it to him.

When she returned the goblet for a third time he set it aside and moved so he was kneeling with his head to her slipper-shod feet. "Your slave is sorry and begs your forgiveness," he stated.

"Who?" Angelique asked.

Jake frowned and lifted himself up onto his hands. "Your slave,

Mistress," he said.

"That would be my choice," Angelique pointed out. "So who, really, is sorry, and what is he sorry for? I can't make a choice without information."

"You know everything about me," Jake began. "Where I grew up, the fact that I dealt drugs for years, that I've been a slave for over five, almost six years now. That's all there is to me, just a slave, after being the lowest of the low," he said.

She just looked at him. Jake groaned and stood up. "Damn! What do you want? Do you want to hear my life story in detail? Do you want me to say I'm sorry that I dealt drugs? Well, my life story is pretty much the same as any poor kid's. And as for dealing and selling, I never forced anyone to buy; they all came to me looking for an escape. I'm sorry that some of them got hurt more in the process, but I never really thought about them. Just about having a roof over my own head and food in my own mouth and a little power now and then."

Angelique stood up. "You're telling me that you didn't have very many choices?" Her voice had a hard edge to it as she spoke.

"They were all bad choices," Jake said. "I just chose the worst of the lot," he paused then nodded. "They were my choices to make and I made the best ones I could."

"So what are you sorry for?" Angelique demanded as she stepped down to stand toe-to-toe with him.

Jake swallowed. "I'm sorry that I couldn't live up to my promise to you."

The green eyes blinked. "But you did. You obeyed me well, as well as you could, I think."

"I returned to your sister," Jake pointed out.

"I never said you couldn't; I simply asked that you obey me as your owner," Angelique replied. She placed one finger against her lips and considered him silently for a moment. "You are a slave by conviction for your crimes. You have served this nation by helping us rid ourselves of a grave threat to all our freedoms and lives. Therefore, I offer you one important choice."

The Queen clapped her hands, and soon the guards entered with a cleaned-up and cared-for Queen Mother and the aristocrats, who'd returned upon word of the Butcher's death. "Jake Monroe, you may go free and leave this country, or you may choose to serve out your life in servitude for your crimes. This will be your final sentence as witnessed by these good folk," she announced loudly.

Jake shifted his weight from one leg to another. "As your slave?" he whispered.

"Of course; you are part of the inheritance," Angelique simply said.

Jake looked around at the faces of the guards and still-frightened aristocracy until his eyes met the Queen Mother's. He turned back then knelt down and looked up at the young Queen. "I've never had anything but my pride. I will not be a coward and run from my sentence. I choose to be your slave, Mistress," he said clearly.

Angelique nodded and clapped her hands again. The blacksmith who'd collared him before entered. His leather and gold collar was removed with metal cutters and then replaced with a thicker one of silver. Each swallow he took made the metal rise and fall. His cock swelled as his head was pushed down by his owner's bedroom slipper. "This slave is mine. No one else may command him but me. Is that understood?"

The crowd murmured their agreement. "Stand up, slave," Angelique ordered when the crowd has dispersed.

Jake rose and focused his gaze over his owner's shoulder. He blinked as her arms moved around him.

"Slave, carry me upstairs now," Angelique said. She sighed as her slave lifted her up into his arms, her back resting against one arm and the other supporting her legs, while hers wrapped around his neck. She turned his head toward her before he stepped out of the throne room. "I'm not my sister," she repeated.

"Mistress?" Jake asked as he looked into her eyes. His entire body was on fire; his pants were ready to burst, and oddly the fear that usually edged everything he had ever done in his life was slipping away with each second their eyes locked onto each other.

"I hope I don't have to tell you what to do once we're upstairs," Angelique said. "If I have to detail every little thing, I'll get bored," she further explained.

The threat was there simply because of her status and his. Underneath it all, she might not be all that different from Yvonne, but only time would tell that. Jake licked his lips. "Would I be allowed to ask questions?" he ventured.

Angelique giggled and tossed her head back so that the bandage on her forehead was visible for just a moment. "Of course, any time you want," she replied. "You can't make good choices without good information. And there will be choices you'll have to make. Those will determine how you are treated."

"Then I hope I chose well, Mistress," Jake replied with a smile and a twinkle in his eyes.

They were up in her suite in a few minutes. Jake laid her on the bed, then stepped back. He slowly removed his clothing, turning his body so she could see everything she now owned. He removed her slippers first so he could lavish his attentions there. He sucked and licked each of her toes until she giggled and pulled back.

Her breasts were as full and soft as he'd imagined them to be. He eagerly put his lips to each nipple and sucked it to a hard little point. Then he turned to her neck as she lifted her head up and back. Her gasps seemed far more real than any he had heard from any woman, and their sound made him harder than he had ever been. Free to do what he wanted to please her, he traveled down her stomach, taut with muscle, and lowered her pants with her assistance.

One glance up into her wide eyes made the permission he was about to ask for irrelevant. He drove between her thighs and worked at the slits and crevasses there. When her thighs grasped his head he took her offered hands and held them as she rolled from one orgasm into another for minutes. He wiped his wet face on the bedding as she settled back down into a relaxed state.

When Angelique touched his head he looked up, expecting a slap or a harsh word. "That was very good, slave," she said.

"Thank you, Mistress," Jake replied. He helped her crawl under the bedcovers, got her a half glass of water, and then went to lay out his mattress at the end of the bed.

Jake never thought to beg for an orgasm himself, and Angelique never offered or teased him unless she intended to bring him to completion.

By choice he was her slave, and by choice she had accepted him. That path meant that other choices were no longer options for either one of them. In the moonlight, the statue of the many-armed goddess on the altar seemed to smile.

Fem Fist Books

Journey Unto Warrior

The dense forest thins a bit as we go further north from our village, which is right on the edge of the unknown land of an ancient nation whose people call themselves Amazons. It has been centuries since any of our villagers saw these people, but tales are still told around the chief elder's home. It is said that a man who sees an Amazon will either die immediately or become the greatest of all warriors in the village.

Don't tell Teucer, but I intend to find one of these mythical creatures, who are said to have the faces of women, the torsos of horses, the arms of the strongest men, and the legs of the swiftest deer, and I intend to return to the village with the body of one. I have only convinced him to go this far because I told him that I spotted a great buck. With our slings and knives, such a capture would make us heroes in the village and be the last step toward manhood and admission to the ranks of the warriors.

My mother and my father begged me not to go, and when I went anyway they predicted dire consequences. They have been farmers for several generations, and while farmers are the backbone of our village, it is the warriors who get the most respect and have their choice of the best girls as wives. Now don't think that I don't want my friend to also be a warrior, but my capturing an Amazon, dead or alive, will guarantee me the fine Penelope for a wife and her handsome dowry for a bridal gift.

Teucer calls to me as I lead him further from the village. "Acron, I have not seen tracks for almost a half mile now."

"Are you afraid to be so far from your mother?" I tease him.

His face reddens, and he increases his pace so that he walks past me. "I am not. I only question whether we will find worthy prey when it gets darker," he says, motioning upward toward the late-afternoon sunlight, barely visible through the dense leaves.

"We will find the buck long before then," I tell him with assurance. "If not today then tomorrow unless you are really a girl who is afraid of the dark," I add.

After a full day's journey we find a suitable spot and make camp. The chief elder and the priest told each of us six boys that we had one week to return to camp with the best game we could capture. The other two pairs traveled south or west, one looking for mountain goats or lions and the others talking of large man-eating fish from the sea. But it is very rare for anyone from our village to travel north, so I used that to convince Teucer to join me. The buck decoy will probably not last much longer.

As though he has read my mind, my friend frowns at me as he looks across the fire he has built. "Acron, what are we really doing up here? The only animals I've seen are tiny ones, hardly the type to get us accepted into the ranks of the warriors."

I sigh and put on my best smile, the one that convinced the fine Penelope to kiss me one festival night, the one that calms my mother and discharges my father's anger when I am late from some lame chore they set me. "I lied, I admit it."

"That's a switch," Teucer mumbles.

"Men don't lie so I will stop lying," I reply as humbly as I can make my voice sound. "What do you think Xuthus and Haemus will bring back?"

"They say they will find the great sea demon and capture him so that our ships may have safer sailing to the southern markets," he repeats with a chuckle. "I suspect they will bring back some big fish or eel and tell us all how much it fought their net."

"Yes, and they will become shipbuilders or farmers if they completely fail," I predict. "And do you think that a mountain lion will be the prize of Comus and Mentes?" He shrugs his shoulders. "Of course not; they could no more capture such a beast than they could the sun. We are both the best of all the youths in the village."

"I'll agree with that," he states as he takes a skin of wine from his backpack. "You have a plan," he adds as he takes a swig then offers me the wineskin.

"I do," I confess, "one which will guarantee us both futures of power and fame."

"Tell me, then," Teucer demands as he pokes the fire so sparks jump into the night air. When I am silent he frowns and promises, "I will not go after Penelope. She's too tall for my tastes, so you need not worry."

"You swear on Pan himself?" I ask. He places one hand over his heart and the other over his groin as he speaks the most sacred oath of our village. "Then I will tell you. We are going to find and capture an Amazon."

The mouthful of wine Teucer had just taken comes out in a shower over the fire, the drops bursting into tiny flames as he coughs. "What? Are you crazy? That's just a myth, a story to frighten children."

"Most myths are based on reality," I tell him confidently.

"Then you are truly mad," he states. "If they do exist, we would die just from looking at one."

"Or we would return with one and become famous," I remind him. "Come on, the finest wife, the best house, the most meat at festivals, and the finest gifts of gratitude on the feast of the warrior." He just narrows his eyes at me and shakes his head. "And if they turn out to be too strong, then we capture something else. Either way we've gone about as far as any living in man in our village has traveled. We'll be heroes," I emphasize, offering him one of the honey cakes my mother, the best cook in our village for many years now, packed for me.

He takes the cake slowly, eyeing me carefully, so I simply continue with my smiling. "All right. Two more days, but then we must turn back. That's all I'll agree to, Acron. I'm not some woman you can charm and trick."

"You're my friend," I reply. "We'll do exactly as you say, Teucer. It was my plan from the start." He snorts as he rolls his eyes and bites into my mother's cake. I'll have to remember to buy her some beads, the fancy imported ones, when I get home.

The forest has thinned considerably as we've traveled for almost two days. Today we have stopped by a river of sweet cool water and are taking a break to plan our next move. I need to convince Teucer to travel just one more day, but I don't have any more honey cakes to aid me. He is already giving me his tired and angry look when we hear a strange sound. I put my hand over his mouth and whisper to him, "Did that sound like women to you?"

He nods with frowning eyebrows, so I remove my hand. "I know to be quiet," he humphs softly. "It did. Do you think?"

"Let's go find out," I suggest. We move cautiously through the low brush along the river's edge to a group of low trees. Crouching there we open the branches just enough to look out onto the water, where the sounds seem to be coming from.

"It's girls," Teucer gasps as he looks at me.

There in the water, which only covers their waists and leaves their ample breasts in view, are two girls of approximately our age. Their hair is dark and wet, hanging down into the water. Their skin is far darker than the skin of any girl in our village, and their arms show muscle as they move, soaping up each other's hair and giggling.

"Who are they?" Teucer asks as he stares.

I can only shrug at first, then smile as I put two and two together. "They're Amazons."

"They don't look like the story," Teucer protests. One of the girls turns toward the trees where we are hidden, so we hold very still. After a moment her friend splashes her with water, and her attention returns to their washing. "Where's the horse torso?"

"Probably just a story," I speculate. "See, they are clearly women, but those muscles, the dark skin — these are women who hunt and fight, like in the tales."

"What about the legs of deer?"

"We'll just have to watch and see," I point out. Teucer smiles and settles down with a lick of his lips. No honey cakes needed now, the gods have provided me with what I needed.

The girls now take turns disappearing under the water several times to rinse their hair. They speak in a strange language, but the giggles are universal signs that under any amount of muscle they are but women. My eyes and Teucer's widen and glance at each other as the girls now move closer to each other and kiss, right on the lips.

"Did you see that?" Teucer asks in a shaky whisper.

I nod silently as my eyes seemed glued to their naked bodies. Their breasts bump against each other and then seem to part and fit together in some manner. Their hands grasp and travel over each other just as mine did with Penelope the night before I left, though her clothing left my imagination running wild and my groin aching. Now their lips part, and they use them on each other's necks and shoulders, taking each other's nipples into their mouths as infants do and as I think about doing often to my future bride.

My hand brushes against the hem of my chiton. Soon I have my hand under it and open my undergarment. I am hot and hard already, so my hand seems to move of its own volition, stroking as the girls' giggles turn to loud moans and cries. A quick glance at Teucer proves him to be in a similar state. In only a few moments we have both sprayed the trees with our come and are panting in anticipation as the girls continue the show.

At first we move back as they exit the water, their arms entwined about each other. We look for their legendary deer legs, but their legs are definitely human, shapely if firm and browned by the sun. They lie right in front of us, completely unaware of us, on towels laid on the riverbank. Their asses are firm and full, their pubic hair glistening with water as they lay down. This close I can see that one is slightly taller than the other. I think of how fine their legs would feel lying over my shoulders as I plowed their fields and planted the next generation.

My cock is firm again, and my hand is still sticky with my earlier spurt. As I renew my strokes, I close my eyes and imagine that Penelope is one of these girls doing this at my orders as a good wife obeys her husband. I obey my eyes as I orgasm a second time and gasp as two green eyes stare back at me.

Teucer and I fall backwards and roll down the slope we had been on as the two girls push through the tress. They stand, their legs and arms wide, the stance of warriors, though they are naked. In their hands, pointed at our now shriveled cocks, are two spears with black heads.

They say something, and when we just stare dumbly at them,

they repeat their words in the trading language of the region. "Who are you? Tell us, or we will kill you here and now!"

Teucer reaches for his undergarment, which is around his knees, as is mine, but the shorter girl slaps his hand with her spear. The gash is sharp and causes him to gasp and pull back, stuffing the wound into his mouth.

"We are warriors from the south," I say, trying to make my voice sound threatening, which is hard when my stomach feels like it's full of cold rocks.

"Warriors?" the taller girl chuckles. She says something to her friend, and their spears come crashing down on our heads. "Some warriors," she says in trade as my vision goes dark.

I hear their voices again in that strange language of theirs before I open my eyes. They are dressed in light armor over chitons with knee-high boots, bows and quivers swung over their shoulders as our tales state. The taller one's chiton is a green to match her eyes and to set off the red curls that fall over one shoulder. The shorter one has hair the color of sunlight and eyes as blue as the sky with a chiton hinting at the color blue, an expensive dye that suggests these girls are wealthy. They both wear bands of leather over their brows to hold back that vibrant hair; at the center of each band is a jewel to match their eyes.

They notice I am awake and come toward me. The taller ones seems attracted to me, for she crouches in front of me, her chiton parting slightly, hinting at the curly hair underneath and the joys of her cunt. She smiles, then suddenly slaps me. I try to swear but discover that my mouth is gagged with something hard. I sniff, and the musky scent of leather wafts up.

"Wake up, boy!" the blonde demands in trade language, pinching Teucer's cheek; he moans and stirs. I can see him very well from my position. He is sitting up against a tree, his arms and legs bent back and tied to it, so he is forced to kneel on the ground. His clothing has been removed, so his cock, sleepy from the blow to our heads, hangs down between his thighs. When his eyes don't open, the girl slaps his cock, causing him to squeak and jerk his head up. In his mouth is a brown leather bit, very similar to those my father uses on the cattle he has turning the mill or water wheel.

I assume that I am bound just like him, since the redhead's hands are now pinching my nipples and I cannot move. At first she is gentle, the tiny flicks and scratches of her nails making my cock jerk a bit and my flesh tingle. Soon, however, she grasps each between two fingers and twists and pulls them roughly until I can feel tears rolling down my cheeks. My skin flushes as I wonder if Teucer can see me.

"Warriors, huh?" the redhead with a chuckle. She twists my nipples in the other direction. "Now what are you?"

"They can't answer, Ocyale," the blonde states. I wonder if Ocyale is her name or a title. "Maybe we should remove the gags."

"I don't need to hear these boys' voices to get what I want," the redhead states. My eyes widen as she lifts her chiton and tucks it into the belt at her waist. The hair there is just as curly and red as that on her head as she spreads her legs. "You wanted to watch, warrior?" she asks. "Well, watch this." She leans back and uses one hand to part her lower lips so that a pink crest is revealed. I am amazed as her fingers stroke up and down, almost as though she had a cock, and the flesh there reddens and grows. Never in my mind did I imagine that women had anything other than the hole for plowing and birthing.

I glance to my left where Teucer is tied and note that his cock is as hard as mine feels. The blonde is also rubbing her fingers up and down her slit. She has tossed her head back and is groaning as she now forms her hand into a fist and pushes into her mound with pounding blows. My eyes, though, are drawn back to the redhead, who is also moaning.

My eyes dart back and forth, catching Teucer's own looks, as I watch the girls pounding into their fists as though they were bulls mating with a cow. In seconds both girls scream and shudder. I wince as the redhead takes her hand from her slit and wipes a slick substance onto my face. The smell of her sex surrounds me, making me dizzy and my cock spasm in desire.

"Is that what you were hoping to see, warriors?" the blonde taunts us as she takes some leaves and wipes herself off. Both girls stand up, lower their chitons and walk out of sight, giggling the entire time.

I glance at Teucer and see that his eyes are closed but his chest is expanding and contracting rapidly. My hands and cock ache as I try desperately to loosen my bonds. The sun is setting by the time my efforts have worn me out. My hands have little feeling as I close my eyes and fall asleep.

A cool breeze makes me shiver, jolting me awake. At first I'm confused; am I blindfolded? The dim stars twinkle as the clouds drift by through the black night sky. I take a deep breath and realize that meat is roasting nearby.

The strange language hits my ears again, getting louder until the redhead is crouching in front of me again; this time she has on leggings, though, so there is no thrill, just fear. She reaches behind my head and loosens the gag so I can push it out with my swollen tongue. I never knew my mouth could be so dry. "What are you called?" she asks in trade.

"Acron," I mutter and try to swallow. My parched throat pains me, so I moan and wince.

The redhead raises her eyebrows, then says something to her friend, who is tending Teucer. The blonde gets up and moves behind me, where the scent of food seems to be originating. She returns and hands the redhead a skin, very similar to the ones we carry wine in. "Drink this," the redhead orders as she opens it and puts the nozzle to my lips.

The water is sweet but frightens me. My people never drink water straight; it can kill a person. But when I try to turn my head, the redhead simply grabs my chin and forces more down my throat until I'm sputtering and water falls down onto my chest.

Teucer, I see out of the corner of my eye, is being more cooperative and even allows the blonde to run her fingers through his hair, still long as a sign that we have not reached manhood yet. I wonder, as I try to swallow as quickly as the redhead tilts the skin, whether we will ever have that honor now.

"Still thirsty?" the redhead asks me when the skin is completely emptied, either into my stomach or onto my naked body. She chuckles when I shake my head. "Good. I'm not your mother," she states as she stands up and walks out of view.

I wait until the blonde leaves as well before whispering to Teucer. "How are you?"

He looks at me, then glances over his shoulder, trying to see where the girls are. "I can barely feel my hands and feet," he whimpers. "I asked Xanthe to loosen the ropes, and she said later."

"Xanthe? Is that the blonde's name?" I ask quietly. He nods and tries to shift positions against the tree. "The other must be Ocyale then." We sit silently for a few minutes, the only sounds those from our stomachs as they yearn for the roasting meat. The girls are chuckling and talking in their language, every now and then throwing in a trade word to frighten us with talk of beasts and dismemberment. I can see sweat dripping from Teucer even though the air is chilly. "Calm down, boy. We have to think, we have to get out of here. They're only girls; we can turn the tables on them."

"How?" he demands with a frightened pout.

I nod and then call out loudly. "Hey, I have to go, now!" I nod to him once more as the footsteps of the girls approach. The redhead and blonde step in front of us, standing with their hands on their hips. "All that water made me have to pee," I explain. Teucer mutters that he must as well when they glance at him.

I try to tense my muscles to bolt the moment I'm freed from the tree, but the girls undo my hands from the tree then push me onto the ground and bind my arms firmly behind my back. When my feet are freed and I'm pulled to my feet by my arms I find them too wobbly to run. I have to groan as I'm led over to another clump of trees; my feet tingle as though a thousand of my mother's sewing needles are being stuck into them.

"Go," the redhead orders when I just stand there.

I look at her, then glance over my shoulder toward Teucer, who is still tied to the tree. The redhead yanks my head around to look at her again. "I need my hands," I try to explain.

She chuckles, as does the blonde. "Horses don't have hands. Just go, warrior," she commands with a rough shake of my head.

At first I feel full of lead; nothing seems to move. "This is the last time we'll get you up, unless you go right now," the blonde states. Suddenly, the thought of sitting in wet grass, smelling my own urine and god knows what else, makes a stream of hot liquid shoot out. I'm weeping silently by the time I'm finished. Teucer turns his eyes away from me as I'm led back to the tree and retied as before.

I try not to watch but find my eyes staring as he is released and led to the same area. If he speaks it is too softly for me to hear, but the blonde once more runs her fingers through his hair. He refuses to look at me as he is led back. Instead of his arms being forced behind him, they are instead lifted over his head and tied off to a low branch so that his elbows can even bend a little. He glances at me, then quickly away as the blonde crouches in front of him and whispers something to him. As I watch her hands touch his chest I feel a cold stone in the pit of my stomach. I feel like I do when my little brother gets to one of my parents before me after something bad has happened, and then I always end up in a ton of trouble and with a bruised backside. After the girls leave, Teucer says something to me, but I turn away and shut my ears.

We have been walking north for several hours, I figure, when the girls finally pull into a meadow and dismount from their mares. They must be very wealthy to have horses. My wrists are raw from where the ropes have rubbed them as the redhead led me forward in jerks, since I just can't seem to move quickly enough for her. Having my feet tied only a foot and a half apart hasn't helped, but every time I bring the point up she's been fast to turn and slap me. My cheek is going to be black and blue in no time unless I figure something out.

Teucer is having a much easier time of it. The blonde has even been talking to him and letting him walk next to her. The redhead kicked me the one time I managed to catch up with her, so I gave up, the worse for my wrists, I fear. Even now, when he should be moving as close to me as he can so we can make some sort of plan, he is following her off toward the woods around the meadow.

"You should behave more like your friend, warrior," the redhead states. She looks at me, up and down, very slowly. My skin feels hot, and I can't meet her eyes. "It can be nice, or it can be hard," she adds. When I refuse to answer, she shrugs and pulls me roughly to her. "Or do you like it hard, boy?"

I glare at her and manage a low growl. This had been enough

to make my mother back off a few years back and even made my father simply yell at me, but the girl just laughs in my face. I move quickly and manage to get a bit of her cheek in my teeth.

Her slap is harsh and knocks me onto my side in the grass and flowers. She stands there wiping the blood from my attack with the back of her hand. Behind us I hear the blonde screaming something. Teucer lands next to me on the ground. "What have you done?" he demands in our own language and groans as the blonde's foot lands on the small of his back.

The redhead glares at me as the blonde screams into Teucer's ear. Out of the corner of my eye I see him flinch as she adds punches to emphasis her points. My own eyes are glued to the green ones of the redhead. This will be the only chance I have; I have to stay calm, I tell myself over and over. I flinch anyway when she crouches in front of me.

"That was very stupid," the redhead states slowly as she wipes her blood under my nose and down over my lips to my neck. I can see the wound and curse at the fact the bleeding has stopped already, it looks like the nip of an angry child. Her hand is like lightning as she begins to slap me everywhere. When her blows start to snap my cock from side to side I try to double over to protect myself.

I feel strong arms pulling me back so I'm laid out helpless, my legs curled under me and my chest thrust up. I look up and see the blonde hair falling over my shoulder as she presses her knee into my back, forcing my exposure further. I turn my head and see Teucer kneeling on the ground, his hands over his face, but he makes no move to aid me. I scream when the redhead kicks my balls with the toe of her boot. She keeps her foot there and grinds them into my body until I would swear they are dust.

Finally I am released and allowed to collapse on the ground. I look at Teucer and try to say something. He reaches toward me, but at the bark of his name by the blonde he jerks back and jumps to his feet. I have enough strength to see him trot toward the girls. I feel sick as they both lightly caress his hair and touch his body.

I'm not allowed to rest long and am soon hurried to my feet and out behind the redhead's horse as we continue the march northward. I walk, this time jogging if she speeds up, even though my entire body aches, and keep my mouth shut and my eyes on the trail under my feet.

The sun is setting again when I notice that the trail has widened enough for the horses to walk side by side. Since I am walking behind the redhead's horse, I can watch as Teucer strolls next to the blonde's horse. I can just make out a few of their words as they talk. I wince as he says "Lady" and earns a grin from her. I feel eyes on me and look up to find the green eyes of my captor staring back at me, then at the others before returning to me. I simply swallow and lower my eyes.

The next day the woods disappear completely, and flat fields of grass replace them as the trail beneath my feet becomes a road like the ones in the big cities our legends paint. The sun is unusually warm for this time of year and makes my skin burn. I'm sure that I have a burn worse than any in my life, especially in my privates, which never see the sun expect for a quick release when I'm hunting or working in the fields. Right now I wish I had a scythe in my hands and my father's stupid jokes in my ears. The dream of being a warrior disappeared sometime last night when I realized that even escaping now would not give us enough time to get home. And without an Amazon to prove our story, we'd be laughed out of the village.

"How are you doing, Acron?" I look up, startled to find Teucer walking next to me. I glance at his hands and find them simply tied in front of him; his feet are free, and he is given a wide range with the lead rope attached to his hands. When I just look at him he glances at the blonde, who nods at him with a set frown. "You were right, you know. They are Amazons, that's what they call themselves anyway."

"They told you that?" I manage to ask even though my hands ache to wrap themselves around his throat.

"Xanthe told me after I told her why we were out here," he begins to explain.

I grab his arm and roughly pull him so his chest slaps against mine and his cock bumps into my thigh. "You didn't tell them where the village is, did you?"

"No!" he states as he pulls free, his lower level of bondage allowing him the leverage not to mention the fact that I saw him eating just last night. I haven't eaten since we were captured. "Look, we aren't getting away from them. These aren't real women; they're more than that; they say they are descended from the gods themselves." I snort, but he continues. "Whatever they are, they're certainly stronger and more skilled than us. Come on, admit it."

"Give in, and be their little pet like you?" I spit out.

Teucer steps back. "Fine, but you take yourself down from now on, Acron. I intend to survive."

I watch him as he strolls back to the blonde and apologizes to her. I expect her to slap him, but she simply sighs and strokes his arm. I feel those green eyes staring at me but refuse to even glance at the redhead. I stumble but quickly recover when she jerks harshly on my lead rope.

"Where are you taking us?" I ask. I'm using my soft eyes and voice this time, hoping that if I can't frighten her I might charm the redhead a bit.

The redhead lifts one eyebrow and crouches down in front of me. She runs her hands up my arms, which are tied to a post Teucer set up this evening at the Amazons' orders. They aren't girls in my mind anymore, but they certainly aren't women either. Well, I smell her musky scent as she leans into me, her breast right before my face; I guess they're women, just not the ones I'm used to .

"Where are you taking us, Lady?" I repeat, adding the title of respect, though it makes me a little queasy.

Ocyale — she told me that was her name when she bound me this morning — backs up and examines my face for a few seconds before answering. "To our city. We'll be welcomed as warriors for capturing such new studs."

I frown, trying to figure out what her words mean. I'm about to ask when a strange sound makes both of us look toward the other two. The blonde, Xanthe, is sitting astride Teucer's thighs; his legs are bent so they support her back; her hands are holding his, which aren't tied above his head or even together. Both of them are moaning and moving, clearly fucking right before our eyes. Xanthe tosses back her hair, and I see Teucer's mouth on her neck.

I swallow nervously as Ocyale looks into my eyes and grins. "Stud," she repeats as she presses her lips onto mine. I gasp, and the parting of my lips gives her an opening, which she widens with her own lips and her tongue. Darting deeper and deeper into my mouth, her tongue makes me melt against the pole. I attempt to return the probing, but she pulls away and stands up.

She laughs as she walks away, leaving me a clear view of Teucer and Xanthe. My cock heaves, but I can do nothing but watch and listen as they both pound and scream until they fall onto their sides. After a few minutes, the blonde gets up and motions to the pole against which Teucer had been sitting. He moves, and I shake my head as he grasps her hand to kiss it before his wrists are lashed to the pole as mine are. He doesn't even glance my way but follows the blonde's every move as she joins Ocyale by the fire. I curse internally, knowing that I can't even move my legs enough to release my own sexual hunger slightly, while I watch him curl his legs up so he can lean back against the pole more comfortably.

The road is now different from any I've ever seen, and I've been to the big sea port two days' journey from our village. The soil is packed down smooth, so tightly packed that the horses barely kick up any dirt. The meadows on either side have become fields of wheat and other grains I can't identify from far away. Every now and then we pass small groups of men in the fields, watched by women sitting astride horses armed with whips. The men wear loose pants but no shirts, while the women are dressed much like our two captors, minus the armor and spear.

My feet started to bleed this morning after we had only walked about a quarter of a mile. It's slowed me down considerably, but Ocyale has no patience with me and simply yanks me down the road whenever the rope gets taut. My knees creak as I fall down on them. The yank on my hands makes me stumble onto my face.

The Amazons says something to each other, then Ocyale dismounts and walks to me. I look up her boots to her leggings, wrapped tightly around her firm, shapely calves and thighs. "What's wrong?" she demands.

"I think my feet are bleeding," I whisper, "and I'm starving," I add. What have I got to lose. If she doesn't feed me soon I won't be alive anyway.

"Get up," she orders. The movement of one of her boots makes me bolt upright, but a kick never lands. She says something to Xanthe, and a piece of fruit is tossed to her. When I reach for it she laughs and takes a big bite.

I swallow as I watch the green flesh part underneath her teeth and a yellowish juice drip down her lip to be flicked up by her tongue. "Lady, please," I hear my voice beg. I watch her closely as she tilts her head and seems to consider my words. She drops the fruit, and I catch it in my hands. "Thank you, Lady," I whisper as I hold the fruit up to my nose and breathe in its scent.

"Come tend to his feet, Teucer," Xanthe orders as I bite into the fruit.

I change my position so I can eat while Teucer picks up one of my feet. "It is bleeding, Lady," he tells them. I hear them sigh, but my eyes are focused solely on the fruit as I munch. Each mouthful is sweet, better, I'd swear, than anything I've ever had before, even my mother's honey cakes. The thought makes my eyes water. "I'll try not to hurt you too much," Teucer whispers as he pours water over my feet and tries to remove some of the dirt and blood.

Once my feet have been cleaned and bandaged and the fruit eaten to the core, Ocyale hands me my boots. I look at her closely, surprised and frightened at the same time. "Put them on. I intend to get you back in one piece, slave," she states.

I frown at the insult but keep my mouth shut as I pull them on. They fit tightly with the bandages, but when I stand my feet certainly don't feel like they are going to fall off at any moment as they did before. Teucer has likewise put his boots on. He looks as ridiculous as I know I must, naked except for boots. In fact, I feel even more naked now with the obvious contrast. They want us for something; it is clearer now than ever.

We travel for several more hours until we see a walled city on a hill a short distance off, near the river I've been hearing to my right. The city is magnificent; the walls look gray, and the towers of the tallest building appear to reach up into the clouds. To our immediate right is a large stone building with a sign hanging from a post by the doorway. Xanthe points to the city and announces, "That is our capital, Themiscyra."

"We'll camp here tonight and enter in the morning," Ocyale says as she dismounts. She enters the building, then returns with a plump woman following her. This woman nods and chuckles when she sees us. She points behind the building with her thumb, and Xanthe, who has also dismounted now, takes both horses' reins and leads them around it. "Come with me," Ocyale orders us.

Teucer follows immediately, but I pause a moment, looking back down the road. I jump when the plump woman touches my arm. She laughs and tweaks my nose. "Come on. Food and water," she says in heavily accented trade language. I have no choice but to follow her now that her hand has wrapped itself around one of my wrists. She's a lot stronger than I imagined.

We are taken around to the back of the building, where the horses have been placed in a stable and are currently being brushed down by a man under Xanthe's watch. We are told to sit down on a bench next to the main building's back door. After being given a bucket and two sponges we are told to wash.

Teucer removes his boots, so I do as well. The sponge feels so soft against my skin; a great deal of the dirt washes off into puddles at my feet. There are two lumps of something soft in the water, and when I place one on the sponge and apply it to my skin it makes a grayish cloud form on my skin. The Amazons chuckle when Teucer and I exchange astonished glances. In our village we use oil and a firm piece of bone to scrape the dirt and sweat off our bodies.

I put the sponge back into the water and am about to release it when Ocyale speaks. "You haven't washed everywhere yet, slave," she says. I glance at Teucer, who is lifting back his foreskin and washing himself very carefully. He also rubs the sponge up and down his shaft and balls, making himself hard. The Amazons nod and mutter their approval when he glances up at them. I let the sponge sink to the bottom of bucket and stand up straight. When Ocyale approaches me I brace for a beating, but she simply pushes me back onto the bench and stands to watch Teucer continue.

My own eyes are fascinated as he dips the sponge back into the water and gathers the gray cloud onto it again. He freezes as Xanthe takes the sponge from his hands. I can't hear what she tells him, but soon he is bent over his hands grasping his ankles and his legs spread wide. My cock twitches as I watch her run the sponge down his back to the crack of his ass. Using one finger she pushes some of the sponge inside him and twists it up and down. To even think of such a thing is forbidden in our village, and yet now I feel myself stirring, and my ears pick up the increased tempo of Teucer's breathing.

"I need to finish," I say softly. Ocyale looks down at me. "Lady, I want to finish," I hear myself explain. She shakes her head and turns away.

I'm tied out in the stable after being fed a meal of porridge and dark black bread. At least I'm sitting in dry, clean hay instead of on the ground. Teucer was taken inside the inn; that is what the building turned out to be. I wonder what he is doing, and almost in reply, to tease me, a few noises that sound a lot like his voice come from inside the house. At first they sound like cries of pain, then soon he is gasping out words in trade, begging and praising the Amazons; finally he says a few words I can't understand but which sound like their language. One of the stable hands, a man about my father's age, stops in his chores to look at me with pity. I growl at him, and he hurries away.

The next morning after a piece of hard cheese and the black bread, I'm told to put a pair of rough pants on and my own boots. My hands are tied in front of me again, but my feet are left free. Ocyale takes hold of my chin, looks at me and sighs. She seems almost sad, so I open my mouth to speak, but she releases me and simply ties my lead rope to her saddle.

I can't help but let my mouth fall open as Xanthe and Teucer emerge from the inn. He is dressed in blue pants, sandals on his feet, and a blue vest with embroidery on it; his hair has been formed into two plaits that fall down his back. From his ears hang two metal hoops. I jump toward him screaming, "You traitor! You fucking bastard traitor!

Woman's toy!"

Ocyale grabs me and throws me to the ground, knocking all the air from my lungs. She stands over me and uses the blunt end of her spear to beat my chest and arms until I'm crying for mercy. Grabbing me by the front of my pants she pulls me to my feet. "You've made your last mistake," she spits at me. She mounts and yanks on my lead rope.

Teucer doesn't even get his hands tied, but at least he is still walking as we head toward the city. I certainly am not going to speak with him for a good long time, and he at least has the brains not to try and speak to me.

The city is bigger than anything I could have imagined. Perhaps they are children of the gods after all. The stones that make the wall are at least as tall and wide as I am and must weigh far more than two oxen could pull. The gates are made of wood with metal bars across and down. It is open to the road, but two guards are stationed there, both women.

Our captors lead us to what appears to be a market. A richly-dressed warrior in armor that gleams like the sun is sitting on a bench on a platform. She motions to Ocyale and Xanthe, and they dismount and approach her, pulling me after them as Teucer steps up willingly. The woman looks at them, then at us, and smiles. She waves her hand, and a horn can be heard blowing. The women and men in the market all grow silent and gather around us. Most of the men are dressed similarly to Teucer now, but here and there, burdened by large packages, their necks encircled by metal collars from which chains fall into the hands of women, are men dressed like me. I swallow, suddenly very afraid.

I look back at our captors to see Xanthe bowing to the armored woman, who must be their chief warrior, and Teucer kneeling, his head bowed, at the powerful leader's feet. He rises and accepts a necklace of tight metal around his neck — a collar, but one that might embrace a beloved pet's neck.

I grunt as I am pulled forward by Ocyale. The chief warrior frowns, then nods. She takes the two offered spears from Xanthe and Ocyale and hands them to another woman dressed in fine armor as well. The two girls smile as they receive swords and scabbards from their chief. They've become warriors, I realize with a twinge of jealousy.

Our captors step off the platform, leaving me alone with their leader and another woman, who takes my lead rope. This woman moves my head from side to side, then speaks to someone behind her. When the metal collar comes into view I try to pull away but am knocked to my knees by the chief warrior's kick to the back of my calves. My heart sinks as I feel the cold metal slip over my neck and the heavy burden rest on my shoulders as it is tightened and locked.

I look at Teucer and his owner, for I realize that we have both been enslaved, though in different ways. He is lifting up his neck as she touches his necklace. His eyes meet mine briefly, and he sighs as though telling me that this is all my fault. At least I still have my honor and have not been reduced to a mere plaything.

There is some shouting for a few minutes, and then a large woman steps forward. She tosses Ocyale a bag that jingles, I assume, with whatever passes as money here. A chain is now attached to my metal collar, and the new woman pulls me off the platform with it. I look back at our captors but turn away when Ocyale's sad green eyes meet my glance.

Later I scream as my new captor beats me, then fucks me with all her strength. My screams soon turn to whimpers as three other women also mount me. One of them forces two of her fingers inside my ass as another gags me with another leather bit. The fingers must have been replaced by another item, for I am soon hoisted to my feet and pushed across a small expanse of ground, but my ass still feels wide and full. In the distance I see other men working in a field. Did I go through all of this only to end up a farmer?

My question is soon answered as I am chained to the spoke of a grinding wheel. My feet are chained to the post in front of me, as are my hands and the lead on my collar. Something is wrapped over my cock and through my legs before being tied around my waist. I scream into the gag as a whip strikes my back sharply. I push and groan but the wheel is soon moving. An older man, humped over with age, lifts a bag and pours grain into the center of the wheel.

As the hours drift by in a haze of pain and humiliation from the guards coming and stroking my cock and pushing the item in my ass around, I find my eyes blurred by tears. When the sun has set and it is very dark outside, the guards unchain me and lead me over to a fireplace, where a few logs are burning. The gag is removed, and I am given a few swallows of water to drink. One of the guards laughs as she kicks my legs out from under me and I land on my ass.

As I sit, my ass full, my movement controlled by the chains and my sore muscles, and eat the tasteless bread I have been given, the face of Penelope forms in my mind. She looks at me and laughs, then I see her go into the arms of Haemus, who is standing in front of a tiny half-built boat. I curse my own pride as I watch the fire burn away the images of my life into the ashes which I have chosen.

I have resigned myself to the harsh life of the mill and the lash. The sexual assaults have disappeared now. I figure that it must have been years, since my beard hangs to my chest and is starting to show a few white hairs. The old man who poured the grain has been replaced by a younger crippled man with light brown hair who speaks the Amazon language perfectly.

A woman with red hair hanging down her back and wearing armor enters the mill one day, accompanied by a blond man in embroidered vest and pants with sandals carrying a red headed tot in his arms. The man stays in the doorway while the woman approaches me. At a word from the guards I stop and stand still. The woman approaches, then waves her hand in front of her nose and stops. My heart falls into my stomach as she speaks. "You never did like to wash, did you, warrior?"

I want to fall to my knees, but the chains and my shock prevent me. I stand silent, chewing on the gag, as Ocyale leaves me to my fate. A tear falls down my cheek as another familiar voice, this one male, comes from behind the door and is joined by that of his own captor. I grunt as the whip snaps into my flesh and my feet push on in their endless toil.

The Captain's Gaze

The water felt so good as it cascaded down his body that Jay tilted his head back further and sighed though lightly closed lips. Three weeks aboard the *Aurora Runner* without another human being's touch was starting to be more than he could handle. The crew spoke to him, he was allowed to wander almost anywhere he wished, he ate at the slaves' table in the officers' mess, and he could access any of the entertainment or literature he wished on the computer. No one touched the Captain's property, however, without her permission, and no one had even asked, as far as he knew.

The water was unexpected aboard a space vessel where everything was either transported or recycled or grown. It was a luxury that everyone on the ship received once a week, Captain's orders. Ten minutes of just relaxing.

Jay bowed his head forward until his brow rested against the one silvery metal wall of the Captain's private shower. Relaxing was not a big requirement for him right now; the shower instead served as a reminder that he was physical, that he was sensual -- in short, that he still possessed all those skills he had used at the brothel on Kortec Nine.

Jay shook himself once violently as the client pulled out of his ass. He rolled his head down, then back and up, as the man stood up and pulled his pants back on. "Thank you, Sir," he stated with a wide grin.

"I think he really enjoyed that," the woman sitting in a nearby chair commented. She was dressed in her uniform, a ship's chief of security by their conversation, and was watching her partner, who was apparently something very high-ranking, called First Officer, get dressed.

"He seemed to enjoy doing you as well," the man answered, giving Jay's ass a light smack as he walked over to the woman.

Jay sat back on his heels; his thighs spread in an open but non-assertive manner, and sighed as he wiped the sweat from his face. "I did, Sir and Madame," he replied with a slight tilt of his head. His hair was damp and plastered to his face, the wet making it darker than it truly was. He'd need a new tinting by week's end, he decided as he waited for his clients' next moves.

The man looked up from his shoes with a skeptical frown. "You just want us to come back and spend more money."

"That's his job," the woman countered as she rose to her feet.

"I really did enjoy it; I enjoy my job," Jay added as he bounced to his feet and grabbed their jackets. He hung the man's over one arm as he held the other for the woman to put on.

"Would you enjoy serving a smaller number of clients?" the woman asked.

"In the same manner?" Jay asked as he lifted the coat's shoulders and adjusted it onto the woman's frame.

"To a degree; other services as well," the man added, just taking his jacket from Jay's arm. "Actually just one client."

Jay licked his lips slowly and lightly as he thought. Private ownership was every slave's dream; the chance for real service or freedom could only be accomplished outside business walls. The second, freedom, held no real appeal for Jay; he'd seen too many freedmen and freedwomen on the streets barely able to find another meal. The first, though, would be wonderful, an opportunity to serve one person so well that the mere thought of it made his skin tingle. The possibility was enticing but perhaps a trick designed to make his heart race then break when the couple never returned or only continued with their hollow promises. He chose to merely smile at the comment.

"It would be aboard a spaceship, a rather large ship owned by a corporation, but the captain is a stockholder, so it is her ship," the woman explained

"You'd be a birthday gift for the captain," the first officer interrupted. Jay only smiled at them, feeling them out, attempting to be ready but not assuming.

"It would be a chance to see the galaxy," the woman added after a few moments of silence.

Jay realized that they wanted him to answer as they stood looking at him. They must have enjoyed his company a good deal to offer him this. He mentally went over the past four hours in his mind. It had been a workout to serve both of them at once then each in turn, because his current clients tended to be very simple and quick; he had hungered for this type of use again. He smiled and gave them the answer they sought. "I would love to serve aboard your ship, Sir and Madame. I would serve very well, and I would enjoy it."

Jay turned and let his back rest against the wall so the water could fall onto his chest. The tiny drops striking his nipples made him moan and clench his hands. He was so horny, hornier than he'd ever dreamed he could be. Some slaves tolerated sexual use, others actively fled from it, and others embraced it as almost a sacred calling. Those in the last group were the most accepting of their condition, and because of corporate and private selective breeding their numbers were growing. It could be hell, though, if one such natural slave were cast out from an owner's favor, because each knew that to touch him or herself without permission was a great sin, a conditioned sin that electroshock therapy had drilled into him.

But time and the water were sorely tempting Jay. He turned his body so the drops hit more directly on his nipples, thrusting his hips out so the water could stream around his arching cock and caress his balls as well. He gripped the wall and recalled his last client at the brothel before being shipped off to this frustrating adventure; at least he'd been touched if not challenged or pleased. In a few seconds his cock was spurting out into the air as he slipped down the wall.

Jay gasped half in horror and half in pleasure as his conscience regained control over his body. He wiped his hair back from his face and opened his eyes. Frozen, he crouched there in the water, his gaze trapped by the Captain's eyes. She was standing there, one hand on her heart, likely in disgust at what she witnessed.

Jay fell down onto his knees and held out his hands. "Mistress, please hear me explain," he called out. He crawled forward to the translucent door as she turned on one foot and exited. "Mistress!" he called after her.

"Damn!" he cursed as he banged his head against the shower door. He'd be touched tonight, but not in any pleasurable way. He sat at the edge of the shower until the automatic timer turned off the stream.

Nothing happened for three days, however -- the same "nothing" that hadn't happened since he'd been presented to the Captain at her birthday party -- until he was summoned to the chief ecology officer in the water reclamation center. The officer motioned for Jay to stand in front of his desk as he took a palm viewer into his hand.

"The captain has made arrangements for you to take a hydro-shower three times a week," the officer stated as he handed Jay the device. "That's your new code, boy; use it well. It's still just 30 minutes total, in 10 minute servings, so don't get all excited."

Jay reread the code several times then handed it back to the officer. "Thank you, Sir," he added as he let his fingers lightly touch the outheld hand. The officer roughly motioned back toward the door and returned to his laptop computer.

Jay couldn't eat that day as he tried to figure out why he was getting more privileges than even the Captain herself. The Captain didn't seem to notice his state of mind as he accompanied her to lunch and dinner but didn't eat anything. Even when he went to sit with three other slaves he knew of that served the ship's officers his behavior was ignored. Regular meals on board ship had required some getting used to, but the haphazard way of living from his brothel past allowed him to miss an entire day's food with no hunger pangs.

That evening, the Captain did something rare; she spoke to him. "Did the ecology officer speak with you today?"

If he had not been looking at her, Jay would have had difficulty identifying her voice. This was maybe the seventh sentence she'd said to him in three weeks? "Yes, Mistress," he replied.

The Captain nodded and started to turn away from him when he spoke up again. "Mistress, may I ask why I was given such luxury?"

He noticed the Captain's cheeks redden a bit before she

laconically replied, "You seem to enjoy showers," then left the main room of her suite to enter her bedchamber, a place he had only visited when she was on duty.

Jay sat up late in his sleeping alcove thinking about the past three weeks. At the Captain's birthday party, everyone but she had been laughing and basically partying. When he jumped out of the cake, Jay was most surprised at the blush on his new owner's face, but soon he was equally surprised at how stoic and distant she was to the rest of the crew around her.

At first he'd performed all the correct greetings but was merely acknowledged by a nod from her. The Captain was an impressive woman. Her dark hair had a few streaks of gray throughout it, her light eyes were slightly almond shaped, and her uniform was filled out nicely. Clearly she was a woman who took her job seriously and therefore took good care of her body.

Jay had either stood or knelt beside her during the evening. At first he had thought that his presence was unusual and that was what was causing her discomfort. However, he had realized about halfway through the evening that he was not the only slave aboard ship but the only one privately owned. Two other categories existed aboard: the officers' slaves and the crew's. Each had a stable of men and women who were available for amusement and to do some mundane work such as cleaning or meal service.

As he remained next to the Captain he found that any attempt on his part to move closer to her caused her to withdraw physically from him. Being unsure of ship's etiquette he couldn't even bring himself to speak to her. Instead he tried to follow her gaze and listen in when she spoke. Her eyes often lingered over the interactions of her crew with the slaves, yet beyond these gazes she seemed content to chat briefly with anyone who approached her.

Attempts over the past three weeks to engage in conversations or offer her physical attentions were politely declined. Jay memorized her duty schedule and her food preferences; he waited silently but within easy reach whenever he was permitted in the same room with her during her off-duty time. She'd spoken rarely and then only to explain the basic privileges and restrictions he had. He had never seen her with less than her exercise gear on. He had never seen more than a slight smile on her face.

When Jay finally fell asleep in his alcove, he continued to piece together everything he'd observed about the Captain. In his dreams he ran scenarios of how he might bridge the gap between himself and his owner.

Jay waited in the hallway outside the First Officer's suite the next day. He bowed when the officer stepped around the corner. While hardly shy during his visit to the brothel, the First Officer seemed skittish around Jay now.

"Does the captain need me?" the officer asked as he moved closer and scanned his retina to open his cabin door.

"No, sir, she did not send me," Jay replied with a flirty toss of his head.

"So why are you here then?" came the anxious reply as the first officer positioned himself in the doorframe.

"I'm hoping that you can tell me how I might acquire a mirror, sir," Jay stated.

"A mirror? I'm sure the captain has mirrors you can use," the first officer replied as he planted his feet more firmly in the doorframe.

Jay smiled as he explained, "One for use in the shower, sir. I think it may improve certain aspects of my hygiene."

The first officer rolled his eyes as though that was far more information that he wished to hear. Jay tried not to frown as the officer called the ship's quartermaster. Everyone on this ship was so conservative, so tightly wound whenever he mentioned the captain. Was there some taboo he was breaking?

"Sir?" Jay replied to the first officer's cough.

"Someone will deliver one to you in a few hours."

"Thank you, sir. If there is anything I can do for you..." Jay offered but was cut off by the officer's stern look. A moment later the door came down between them.

As he walked down the hallways, Jay wondered if leaving the brothel had been a good move. Things on Kortec Nine had been much simpler.

Before the captain was off-duty, Jay adjusted the mirror's angle to just the right position so that he did not appear to be looking at it but could use it to watch the entryway where she had stood before to watch him. He had had some very conservative clients in his time. By comparing the captain to all of them, he had figured out what he hoped was a great plan to help her break down those walls and reach out to claim what was hers.

The first attempt failed.

Jay reasoned that it was because he just flat out pleasured himself as he checked in the mirror to make sure the captain was watching him. He could overcome his conditioning a bit by having an internal dialog with her and pretending he was obeying her orders, but she couldn't hear those thoughts; she could only see that he was transgressing a fairly old tradition. Instead of her usual blush she turned white, her mouth hanging open slightly until she turned on her heel and walked out of the bathroom entryway and out of her suite.

Clearly the captain had extra servings of conservativism if he had only been smart enough to judge by her previous interactions with him. It had been a foolish attempt and had resulted in even fewer interactions with the captain than he had previously imagined possible. At least Jay could say he hadn't foolishly drawn attention to himself when it happened. No, that mirror's angle needed to be kept a secret if this was going to work at all.

This evening would be different.

Jay sat quietly on the floor across from her as the captain ate dinner then read the week's Universal Times. When he determined that she was within a few minutes of finishing the news, he gracefully rose to his feet and announced, "With your permission, Mistress, I'll go take a shower now." The captain glanced up at him and nodded her head.

He'd re-measured the mirror's angle earlier to work with his new scenario. If this worked, if she gave him any positive reaction at all, he'd learn some very important information about her. If this didn't work, well, there was always the more direct approach but he doubted that would do much more than get him sold at the nearest auction.

First he did a regular quick clean, keeping one eye on the mirror.

He was just rinsing his hair when he saw her peer around the door. As soon as all the suds were washed away he jerked his head back and fell to his knees. "Forgive me, Mistress," he said to the wall directly opposite her. She stepped back a bit with a glance at the mirror then took two steps slightly further into the entryway.

"Only by your order, yes, Mistress, I understand," he said softly as he contorted his face as though in pain. She took another step and now had crossed the line into the bathroom.

Jay jerked his head down as though it were being tossed. "Now?" he whispered and was rewarded with the captain's advancing a few more steps.

"Where?" he asked. Slowly, as he asked for imaginary instructions, Jay touched his body. The touches were varied; a soft stroke along his stomach, a sharp pinch of his nipple, a sway of his neck, then a snap to one side when he slapped himself.

He monitored each act by watching her reactions in the mirror. As he stroked his cock for the third time after another resounding smack on his ass, she stepped up to the shower and reached out with one hand to very lightly touch the glass.

Jay tore his hand away and pressed it against the metal wall as he begged, "Please." The captain stepped back, her face flushed, and exited quickly.

The next sound wasn't pretending as Jay leaned against the metal as the water turned off with a beep of the timer. He chuckled softly and willed his erection away. "A few more ought to do it," he speculated as he glanced back toward the entryway.

Watching her watching him was turning into quite an educational experience. First, while she seemed to like the rough stuff, it worked best when he pretended that he was resistant to it or that it was nasty or punishment. That could be a problem because as much as Jay liked role-playing, a good old-fashion fuck was wonderful.

Second, being more aware of her when he was in the shower turned into his being more aware of her watching him at other times. She did indeed note when he moved around the mess hall or spoke with others. However, she seemed intrigued when he managed to make physical contact with another officer, crewmember, or slave and not displeased. No one aboard this ship was going to believe that, Jay realized quickly as he was pushed aside, hushed up, and even just ignored.

The most important thing he learned was how much she liked words. That was the biggest surprise, considering how very little she herself talked. With each new shower session, each time he caught her watching him dress, he started adding in dialogue, but speaking more quietly, and thus forced her to get a bit closer to him each time. On the last few occasions she had even silently mouthed some words to him.

Jay paused in his shower fantasy and leaned slightly back toward where the captain was crouched next to the stall. "Please, Mistress, please tell me what to do," he whispered.

He willed his body to tremble slightly, his engorged cock swaying heavily as he moaned. "Please, its so hard, so hard. Please, pity, Mistress," he whispered again.

The seconds of silence dragged by and he was about to continue with the scenario when he heard her whispered reply. "Touch it." Inwardly Jay was gasping; her voice was deep and husky, sexy beyond what he had imagined; outwardly he just ran his fingertips along his shaft and trembled more.

"How?" he whispered back after a few more silent seconds. Half opening one eye he noticed the captain glance around a bit nervously as though she was at a loss for what to say. "Soft, rough, please, Mistress, anything, please," he moaned back with an extra tremble of his lips and free hand.

The captain swallowed then nodded once. "Softly, at first," she added, biting her lower lip.

Jay ran his fingertips up and down his shaft, at times making a loose ring of fingers and thumb to encircle it. He had allowed himself no cheating once this seduction began, so within minutes he felt close to the edge as he balls tightened. "Please, Mistress, so close, please let me come."

She blinked at him a few times and glanced at the mirror. No, she couldn't tell he was watching her, because he'd worked very long to make sure he knew exactly how to angle his body and the mirror. The captain nodded.

"Please, tell me, Mistress," Jay couched softly. "Order me to come, please," he added after a second.

The captain pressed one of her palms against the glass so it was at about the same level as his cock. Her gaze swept up his body then back down before she whispered, "Come."

Jay played every feeling that shot out of his balls, along his shaft and out into the air with loud moans and gasps of "thank you." The captain waited only a second before moving to rise, so he said quickly, "Thank you, Mistress. That was one of the best ever," he added without moving his head from where he gazed up at her imaginary image standing above him. The real captain paused and a slight smile tugged at her mouth before she left the bathroom.

Once he'd come, Jay's body desired more, so it took him several minutes to get relaxed and under control. She had interacted with him this time, and she'd heard him interact with her; he could not and would not risk ruining that advancement over his groin's demands.

Several repeats of similar situations occurred over the next few weeks. Each one did indeed increase their interactions, but each also made Jay more horny and less patient. At this rate she might touch him in a year's time, he darkly calculated. No, he needed to push things farther; he needed to risk breaking his secret observations.

First he needed to create a desire in her too, so he did not take a hydro shower for four days. On the fifth she put down her news and spoke to him. "Is there a problem with the hydro shower?"

Jay sighed and bowed his head. "I'm ashamed to admit it, Mistress, but I can't figure out how to make it work correctly."

"What?"

"It seems to have stopped working as well as it was before," he added. He waited to follow until she was on her feet and on her way into the bathroom. He watched her tinker with the controls, then announce that it worked. "I think the mirror may be the problem," he suggested as he stepped into the position she normally took.

The captain rolled her eyes and crouched down to examine it. Jay just watched as calmly as he could as her attempt to look at herself in the mirror showed only him standing outside. He fought every instinct to bolt so he could remain still as she stood up and turned to look directly at him.

"You know," she said softly.

"I like it," Jay replied as he stepped to the door of the shower. "I like it more when I hear your voice." He stepped onto the doorframe. "I'd love it if you could instruct me, Mistress." He stepped into the shower, directly in front of her.

They stood there for several seconds as the captain seemed to shrink inside before reconnecting to reality again. "I have the right," she whispered.

Jay blinked. That was not an expected answer, but he quickly regained his composure. "Yes, it is your right, Mistress."

"It isn't wrong," she added.

"Yes, it isn't wrong, Mistress."

"Because you're just a slave," her voice sounded very unsure.

"No; because I'm your slave, Mistress." Jay looked her directly in the eyes and she seemed frozen for a second. "Just yours," he added.

This crossed a boundary in her mind, and the captain smiled slightly as she moved toward the stall door. Jay stepped aside but kept his eyes on hers.

The captain told him softly to remove his clothes, and he laid them on the floor outside the shower. Then she nodded at the shower, and he turned it on. At each order he repeated the words she used and narrated how he complied.

"Mirror," she said, as she held out her hand in the slightly open stall. Jay looked at it, then at her, before retrieving it from the wall.

"Mirror. I give you the mirror; you control my gaze," he added as he handed it to her. Their hands touched, and she didn't pull away but held the mirror with him for a while. "Yours," Jay confirmed.

"Mine," she said, and with her words and his, made it so.

Doll

Harry rolled his eyes, watching the shirt fly across the room and land somewhere off to his side. "This won't work; neither will this, or this, or this. What is this, two years old?" With each comment another piece of clothing went sailing from the closet and onto the floor.

When she was done with her yearly rant her closet would be nearly empty, and the local Goodwill would see a miniature flood of haute couture in circulation. The maid was picking up each item with a smile on her face. With each passing year Barbie — yes, that had been her real name before she'd joined the team — seemed less worried about the outburst. She'd take care of the old stuff; Harry's job was the shopping.

Harry waited until the clothes stopped floating through the air to step around the dressing screen. There she was: her porcelain skin perfect, her blonde hair in its boyish bob, and her crystal blue eyes pouting as much as her perfect mouth. She was dressed in one of her oldest garments: a silk robe from the Second World War, a gift from one of her servants who had died a few decades later. She turned to him and shrugged. "I'm completely out of fashion, Harry, darling. You will fix this, won't you?"

"Of course, My Lady. You know I have been waiting merely for your permission to bring you the finest couture available," he said as he stepped closer. Almost on cue he opened his arms so she could cuddle into them. "Consider this a nice vacation. You don't have to go anywhere unless you want to; just relax, I'll take care of everything."

He had been taking care of everything now for nine decades. Emma Metcalf had been a rising model in the early 1920s when she met the creature of the dark that would become her agent and then her creator. Harry had been in charge of her makeup and wardrobe at the modeling agency, and they'd gotten along so well that she had confided in him one evening after the photographer yelled at her for her insisting on evening shoots only.

At first Harry merely played into what he knew had to be fantasies, but as he accompanied her to various locations he learned what she had become. A few years ticked by, and then the stock market crashed, sending her and her creator into a panic. After he'd found them all a place to stay and made assurances that their comforts would be met, she'd been allowed to give him her blood. It wasn't for love that Harry had stayed with her before those fateful feedings; no, he was purely interested in women as fashion plates, while other masculine forms stirred his less-refined desires. That had changed when he'd taken her blood. Now she was all he could dream about, awake or asleep.

"I know, I know," she muttered against him as she soaked up his body heat. "How long do you think it will take?" she asked as she stepped back.

"As long as necessary, and not one second longer," Harry promised with a smile. "Of course, I know you; you've been looking at magazines, watching the runways on the television. You must give me some guidance, Emma," he cooed at her.

"That's your job," she started to tease as she playfully pulled away.

"Please," he asked as he kept her one hand in his and raised it to his lips. "Hints would be very helpful."

"Maybe," she said, rolling her lovely eyes as she placed her back against the empty closet wall. "I think I need some inspiration, though." Her voice was a bit husky now as she pulled him after her.

They fell to the floor with her pinned beneath him. "I can inspire you," he stated firmly before parting the silk covering her. The perfection of 19 very well-bred years lay before him as he lowered his lips to each part of her. Her cold skin heated up under his mouth and teeth; she squealed as he bit down, taking tiny samples of her blood.

"Go lower," she said, softly spreading her legs for emphasis.

He loved this part most of all. The neatly-trimmed pubic hair was pale blonde and held her scent, the metallic tinge of blood, and the fragrance of her delicate custom-made soaps. "Emma," he moaned into her skin before spreading her lips gently.

"I'm not inspired yet," she giggled and started to close her legs.

A bit roughly he used one shoulder and one hand to keep her spread, but her resistance was momentary. Some of her kind needed the pain and the struggle, usually from their victims, to get truly aroused, but she was perfect in all ways, so the playfulness was all that was required.

Now it was his turn to tease, so he dipped lips and tongue quickly up and down, in and out, moaning words about how beautiful and delicious she was as he worked. Once upon a time he'd heard that all women faked arousal and orgasm, but she had no reason to do so, and when she finally started flexing her thighs and gently bucking beneath his mouth he knew he was starting to inspire her.

Burying his face now between her thighs and opening her up further, he was rewarded with several spurts of her blood. For some reason this blood always tasted sweeter, more vital, more alive, than that from any other spot on her body. Harry cringed a bit as he felt her fingers wind in his hair to hold him down for one final thrust. Gentleness was by far what he preferred as well.

Then he crawled up to hold her as she giggled some more. "So what have you a fancy for, My Lady?" he whispered when she nipped at one of his fingers and sucked down a bit of his blood.

She saw her eyes wander down to the silk beneath and around them. "I'm bored with Europeans, Harry," she stated. "I still have not forgiven the Americans for those dreadful sixties," she added, and her voice held as much anger as he'd ever heard from her.

"There are a few Asian shows soon. I'll go there and find something that will highlight your grace and beauty. Perhaps Barbie would like to come with you and you both can enjoy yourselves while I do all the work," he replied. To show her joy in his decision she turned his head and took his blood directly from his neck, the contact and the pressure making him shoot in his trousers as he moaned.

Harry closed his list up and returned it to his briefcase. Between five shows around Asia ranging from India to Tokyo, he'd found a suitable wardrobe for the next year, or perhaps a bit longer, since he'd focused on more classical styles. His own suits and outfits had been ordered already, since he knew the colors that worked best for her and his goal was to compliment her as any good accessory would.

He glanced at his watch for a moment then headed toward the designer contacts, flashing his pass as he went. He had multiple copies of Emma's measurements, because she found standing for them tiresome, and the price they were willing to pay had yet to fail to overcome the reluctance of any seller. They might design the clothes, but she made them look wonderful; they'd be honored to have her in them when they saw her picture.

Emma and Barbie were off sightseeing, following the schedule he'd arranged to help the lady relax and keep them away from the shows. This was his job, and once he'd chosen the shoes, the undergarments, and the makeup he could start planning out each outfit for the several dozen events she was already scheduled to attend when the new year arrived. A few highlights in her hair and changes to her makeup, a modification of her name, and a few years of solicitude every decade or so had hidden her identity well. Mortals were so willing to not see what was right in front of their eyes.

Ordering took another three hours, and then he could sigh and relax in a nearby area designed just for that. He checked his cell phone finding one message from her. She was bored; they'd try the theater as suggested, but he shouldn't be surprised if they arrived a bit early. Harry looked around but didn't see them, so he headed toward the check-in to retrieve his coat so he could wait outside.

"She still allows you so much freedom." A masculine voice made Harry stop and turn around.

The owner of the voice was standing next to one of the curtained alcoves that lined the sales room. The pale gentleman seemed a bit familiar. "Excuse me?" he inquired, stepping a few feet closer.

"It's only been four decades, boy; you don't remember me?" the man asked as he stepped back a few steps. His eyes were dark and piercing, they seemed to dig into Harry's mind and soul, taunting him with something deep inside. This close he could see that the stranger was one of her kind; reason dictated he should exercise extreme caution but something else was competing with rational thought.

Harry frowned. "Four decades is a long time for me, Sir," he added and stepped closer. Again something in the back of his mind was hinting that this was dangerous, but he found he couldn't tear his eyes from the stranger's dark ones.

"And for her, too, I imagine. Upstart," the stranger growled as he stepped behind the curtain but held it open for Harry, who entered. "Drop the briefcase," his attacker hissed.

Harry felt his fingers relax and heard the leather case hit the floor and his foot. He should resist, he really should. "I have to go now; I'm sorry, I really can't talk …"

"Silence," the now oddly familiar creature ordered.

Harry found his attempts to speak met with swelled lips, a dry throat, and a burning in his chest. He fumbled with his cell phone for a few moments before he was ordered to drop that too. He groaned silently as his knees hit the floor next, and the bastard's cold hard dick was presented to him.

It was the ugliest and most horrifying thing he'd seen in decades, and yet something was stirring inside of Harry as he tried to look away, tried to forget something that seemed right on the other side of his mind. Another silent groan as his head snapped to the side from the stranger's slap.

"You do not turn away from me," his attacker growled. "I remember your insult at the Beverly Hills party four decades ago. You both thought you could hide from me? Now I'm going to have what you refused me, bitch."

Beverly Hills party? Harry remembered several of them, but not this guy, not this monster. He focused all his willpower on resisting the order to open wide, but found his mouth impaled nonetheless.

His attacker could silence him and make him kneel, but he couldn't keep the tears from falling from Harry's eyes as he vainly fought off the commands and felt his throat penetrated over and over again, choking each time but not allowed to gag by the monster's mind control.

"You know how to do this, bitch; don't act like you don't. Work me good, or you'll regret it," his rapist growled. It was like a nightmare. Harry's hands rose and started to caress the monster's balls and ass as best they could from his position. His tongue lapped at the underside of the cold cock, and he was even allowed to pull back to tickle the obscene head before deep-throating again.

Harry's tear-rimmed eyes swept down as he felt his trousers grow a bit tighter. The rapist noticed too, and laughed as he thrust. "See? You love it, bitch. You waste your time with that whore. You should be sucking on this every night. You know you want to. Your kind don't change, no matter how many mind games get played."

Then the movement stopped, and Harry found his mouth full of ashes. He coughed, blinked and become more aware of his surroundings.

"Excellent kung-fu moves, My Lady." That sounded like Barbie's voice, so he focused in that direction. Yes, it was her, and she was now sipping on a drink in a Styrofoam cup.

"Not too silly? I was worried about the yell." That was Emma, and she now stepped into his line of sight. His eyes were playing tricks on him because it looked like she had a wooden stake covered in ashes in one hand.

"Oh, no, I think it was just enough," Barbie insisted, followed by another slurp of her drink.

Emma was smiling at him now, her perfect eyes a bit sad. "Well, that was not what I was hoping to find when you emergency text-messaged me. You're lucky we were only a block away."

"My Lady, I don't know who he was; he said something about Beverly Hills, but I don't know him, I swear," he began, but she put two perfect fingers over his lips.

"There's nothing to remember," she told him firmly, and he felt images, words, tastes, and textures burn away. "You tripped and dropped your briefcase, and we found you." Each word revived a mental motion picture as though this were a repeat of some event from his past. "But I do need your help, because I've broken a fingernail."

Then she stood up as his vision swirled and straightened out. In the distance he heard a snapping sound, then a squeak of displeasure that made him look up at her. "I've broken a nail. Look at this," she whined as Barbie fussed over her.

Harry scrambled to his feet, his knees tender from his fall. It didn't matter, though, as he opened his briefcase and found the manicure kit. "Let me take care of that, darling Emma. I'll take care of everything." Behind him Barbie was slurping on some drink, clueless again on how to behave in such a setting.

"I know you will, Harry; you always take such good care of me," she cooed as she offered him her damaged nail and kicked something behind her that he couldn't really see though it smelled a bit like ash that floated away as quickly as the brief thought of them did.

About the Author

TammyJo Eckhart, a dominant sadist, has been consciously active in the BDSM community since 1993 when she moved to NYC to pursue a master's degree in ancient history at Columbia University. There she became involved in TES (The Eulenspiegel Society) on a semi-regular basis as well as helping found the Columbia University group, Conversio Virium (1994-1997) where she served as Treasurer, Health  Service Committee Chair, and finally as Spokesperson. From 1995-1997, she hosted the Applemunch, a monthly dinner for those interested in BDSM living near Manhattan, NYC. For five years (1998-2003) she was the education coordinator for the Indiana University group, Headspace. Her non-fiction has been published in Laura Antoniou's *Some Women* (1995) and in the journals <u>SandMUtopian Guardian</u> and <u>Prometheus</u>. Her fiction has appeared in anthologies from Circlet Press (*SM Futures* (1995)), Greenery Press (*Dreaming in Color* (2003)), and Blue Moon (*Color of Pain, Shade of Pleasure* (2004)). Four collections of her own femdom erotica are have been published. *Punishment for the Crime* (1996) and *Amazons* (1997) by Masquerade Books, *Justice* (1999) by Greenery Press, and *Eroscapes: Erotica from the mind of TammyJo Eckhart* (2004) by Wells Street Publishing. In her writing and in real life, she has been told that she shatters the common stereotypes of dominant women. She has also selectively trained would-be submissives or slaves and mentored some new tops and dominants. As of the winter of 2006, her "kinky family" is comprised of Tom, her husband since 1992, and Fox, her slave since 1999. Currently she is the featured book reviewer for KinkyBooks.com who occasionally takes her to conventions each year. She has presented workshops and lectures for college groups and regional conventions for several years. Please feel free to visit her website currently at http://www.kiva.net/~teckhart.

www.ingramcontent.com/pod-product-compliance
Lightning Source LLC
Chambersburg PA
CBHW071229260626
47162CB00004B/1475